Hell's Back Door

Stark City was a hell-hole of a prison set amongst countless miles of desert and run like a feudal stronghold by the vicious Captain Hector Stark. And amongst a motley bunch of murderers and criminals of every kind there was the legendary Clay Dachin, an educated man but reputedly a cold-eyed killer.

No prisoners had ever escaped and survived but Clay was determined to break the pattern and gathered a formidable bunch of men around him. But could they escape and even if they succeeded, could they beat the relentless desert?

Or would Clay, like an earlier prisoner, end up with his head stuffed as the Captain's trophy? Only time would tell.

Hell's Back Door

Vic J. Hanson

A Black Horse Western

ROBERT HALE · LONDON

Robert Hale Limited
Clerkenwell House
Clerkenwell Green
London EC1R 0HT

Typeset by
Derek Doyle & Associates, Liverpool.
Printed and bound in Great Britain by
Antony Rowe Limited, Wiltshire

Part One

THE PIT

ONE

Stark City. A prison in the wilderness. Not, of course, a large city, but a walled, captive one, grey, forbidding, *quiet*. Like a large adobe fort that had been sacked by Indians but not burned, the dead left behind.

There were no women or children, though, in Stark City. No dead men either, only those who figured they might be better off dead, or in some other kind of hell.

Beyond those grey walls of impregnable thickness there were countless miles of desert; more hell; with no cover from the blazing sun, no water, no humans or help.

Oh, yes, men died. By their own hands or by others. And they were taken past the grey walls and out to the burial grounds and hidden and covered by rocks. Predators roamed outside the walls and howled at the thick, wooden, iron-studded gates and birds screeched in the skies above.

But this was only at certain times when the predators thought there might be pickings. And there seldom were – and the predators fought among themselves and swooped and chased each other back to places where there was food and shelter.

The human denizens of Stark City had food and shelter, but little else. Discipline was strict and there were whippings and human incarcerations and occasionally a hanging or death brought about by feuds among the prisoners themselves. Most of the inmates were from the Southwest and the hill countries and feuding was their nature.

But there were some who, for the most part, kept to themselves: strictly dangerous ones the others left alone.

And Clay Dachin was one of these.

About him rumours were rife.

He was a killer who had fourteen notches on the walnut butts of his twin guns. But nobody had seen those guns.

He had run with the border *comancheros* and was a womankiller.

He had killed a husband who had caught him with a wife and he had set the house ablaze over their heads. It was said there had been children there also.

He had killed a county sheriff and two deputies before being overwhelmed by a posse. They could have lynched him, but they hadn't. In Stark City there were other things murmured about him. Terrible things. It was said that he bore a charmed life, that he always escaped.

But he hadn't yet tried to escape from Stark City.

New inmates were told about him and might have thought he bore horns and a forked tail and could've been surprised when they saw him first. A tallish, straight man about thirty years old, cleanshaven and with the cropped poll that was obligatory to all inmates.

They sidled closer to stare at him, and then he looked at them and they saw his eyes.

As a rule, men kept their eyes down, particularly when warders were near, for they soon took umbrage at what they called 'insolence': they carried stout canes as thick as clubs and liked to use these freely. They had been picked for their task and had been picked well.

The new fish were surprised and startled to learn that, unlike the others of longish-standing, the legendary Clay Dachin looked at everything straight and had the bluest and coldly chilling eyes you ever saw.

They did not approach him, the new fish. They saw him speak to people in passing but nobody seemed actually to approach him. They wondered whether he had some understanding with the warders, the sadistic guards. Or maybe the guards were as superstitiously wary of him as were his own kind. But what was his own kind?

The borderlands were full of loners. But this was a loner to end all loners – and in such an environment too!

It was said that, despite his horrendous reputation, he was an educated man and that he was allowed paper and pen in his cell and was always writing. He had no cell-mate but those in his corridor said they thought he was writing a book.

Still, he was their *celebrity* and they wove tales around him and surreptitiously bathed themselves in the evil glow of his notoriety.

Those who had heard him speak said he was articulate and courteous and had a flavour of the Deep South about his speech and his manner. And another legend grew. That he was a son of a rich Southern plantation owner, and he had gone bad and run to the West as many of his kind did.

Maybe the war had brought the plantation to ashes and turned him into a wild dog. But there was nothing wild about him; and there was another enigma!

Everybody wondered what the Cap'n knew about him, whether the Cap'n knew the truth of him.

Captain Hector Ezekiel Stark, who had given this walled city of misery and mystery its name and ran it like a medieval emperor with the power of life and death over his serfs and his peons and, backed by a small army of specially picked big men, used his powers extensively.

He was a Southerner, was supposed to have served the Confederacy. Eastern power, the power of the victors, had given him this job, however, and left him to accomplish it at his will. Who back there cared what happened to miscreants in the 'Wild West'?

He had his power, the ultimate. And he had his extras; thought of them as that, all part of the tremendous warp and woof of his power. He was an unimaginative man and never thought that he might just be a fish in what was but a small dirty puddle in the far-reaching land of the great USA.

He controlled his own supplies, using the money allocated to him by the powers-that-be, those that he didn't think of as powers all. They had no power over *him*!

He got his supplies from sources that told him nothing and he asked them nothing. They came from the edge of the borderlands and from over the big Mexican river, came usually in covered wagons drawn by mules driven by muleskinners who were of every persuasion peculiar to the borderlands: Mexican, Indian, renegade American, *mestizo, vaqueros*, army deserters, *bandidos, comancheros*, the scum of the desert and the beaten earth.

He had Civil War cannons on his battlements and white men with rifles who shot straight and always shot to kill. The border dealers, with their cattle and their goods respected the Cap'n – and they loved his money: the Mexicans and the Indians loved it most because they knew it was Anglo–American whether it came in gold or scrip. They had no reason to fall out with the Cap'n and his crew.

It was well known along the borderlands that not long after Stark City was built and filled with the most lawless bunch of criminals imaginable, there had been a break-out and six men had gotten away into the desert.

The thing had been well planned. They had horses, weapons, grub, plenty of well-filled canteens. They were led by a guard who had concealed his ex-outlaw identity, had, for a handsome reward, planned the whole thing.

He had fooled his warder friends and his chief,

Captain Hector Ezekiel Stark. But he had not reckoned with the folks outside who were the Capn's friends and allies and co-conspirators in fraud against the distant powers-that-be.

A wagon train was crossing the badlands with supplies for Stark City. Even the ex-outlaw guard leader of the escapees had not known that supplies were due, that was a thing that the Cap'n had always kept strictly to himself: times, places, weights, additions, sometimes a small herd of cattle for butchering, or a bunch of squealing pigs.

This particular train had no livestock, but it had everything else that the Cap'n had reported he needed, and the train was guarded by a bunch of quick-shooting renegades.

The renegades and the prisoners fought a battle. The prisoners were outnumbered and, although they had weapons and a store of desperation, they had been weakened by their deprivations.

They were all killed and left lying for the buzzards and other predators. The head of their leader, known by the muleskinners and the gunfighters as a guard, was hacked off and taken back to the Cap'n for a trophy.

He had it stuffed by a prisoner who had once been a taxidermist. The grinning head now had a place of honour on a specially carpentered plinth in the lobby of the warders' place of recreation near the main gates where everybody coming and going could see the Cap'n's trophy.

A grisly and horrible reminder. A signal to all of the power of endless pain and the power of death

that lay with the Cap'n, his minions and their border-
land friends.

.

TWO

'Dachin's in there all right,' said Jigger.

'We'll have to get him out then,' said Peaboy.

'If I know Dachin he'll be workin' on that hisself,' said Jigger. 'But nobody'll know anythin' about it till he's ready.'

'Darn tootin',' said Bruke who hadn't spoken till then. He was the muscle, not the brains. He was the eldest of the trio also and sometimes referred to the other two as 'whippersnappers', a word he'd picked up someplace and was mighty proud of. He didn't usually run to many words.

Bruke was smart enough to figure that Jigger and Peaboy weren't quite as old as Clay Dachin, but already were beginning to spout like they thought they were a whole lot smarter than Clay. After all, Clay was in jail and they weren't.

Bruke didn't figure it this way, knew that Clay Dachin was the smartest cuss he'd ever known. He wanted Clay out, though, and was willing to go along with anything the two boys planned.

Jigger, small and brown and fast. Like an Injun.

14

Peaboy, taller, lean but muscular, though not as powerful as Bruke. Jigger greased lightnin' with a gun but probably not as fast as Clay. Peaboy, a joker with a knife.

Still, all three of them were pretty good with any kind of hardware – and they had no scruples whatsoever.

Jigger said, 'Caliero is right on the border an' is not very far from Stark City I guess, though there's the badlands in between.'

Peaboy whooped and slapped his thigh.

'Hell's bells,' he said. 'That border hole! Hell's Back Door all right. We oughta be able to pick up some more boys there.'

'We'd need more *dinero* for that.'

'We'll get some then. We'll go see Panama Jack. He'll be able to steer us to somep'n. For his share o' course.'

'An' we take the chances while he sits on his bony ass,' said Jigger. 'Man, I don't trust that damn' skelington at all.'

Both men looked at Bruke who said, 'We gotta get Clay outa that place, don't we?'

Clay Dachin was a model prisoner, although the reverse had been expected by warden, warders and inmates. It almost seemed there was a sort of truce between the notorious killer with the set face and the bright, cold-blue eyes and the bully boys who ruled the captive city.

It was bewildering and frustrating to some inmates that this state of affairs continued. They wanted

15

something to blow and they would've joined in if something had. But it didn't.

And still they walked around Dachin as if he was surrounded by thorns. They spoke scathingly to each other about what they thought was his lack of initiative. But they said nothing to his face. There were those, though, who affirmed that he just must have something secret going, was biding his time.

What none of them knew – and maybe none of the warders either – was that the Cap'n hated Dachin, had wanted Dachin to kick-up, so that he (the great and powerful emperor of all) could cut the man down for all to know about, maybe eliminate him altogther.

It was sort of cat and mouse, and the cat was becoming frustrated, vicious. Then Mad John Mulooney was sent to Stark City, and the cat had his chance and pounced upon it.

Mad John had, with a long-handled woodman's axe, killed his own family and that of his neighbour too. He shouldn't have been sent to a normal jail but incarcerated elsewhere or destroyed like the mad animal he was, a beast who enjoyed killing. In his quieter moments he was a large, shambling man with a boyish face, a demeanour which may well have saved him from the hang-rope.

In the block where Clay Dachin lived, a block that housed supposedly dangerous prisoners with a single cell each, there was an empty space. A man had been released. The Cap'n put Mad John in the empty cell.

Near here there was a clear area where these men could stroll and there Clay Dachin met Mad John.

It was learned that Mad John was a Southerner, as was the Cap'n and, it was thought, maybe Dachin was too. Dachin and Mad John called together briefly – they were both taciturn – but courteous as Southern gentlemen were supposed to be.

Maybe the Cap'n was sort of watching on the sidelines, but nobody saw him. Guards kept a wary eye on the two dangerous prisoners, however. The big shambling man and the other, leaner but almost as tall, who walked like a cat.

Maybe it hadn't been a good idea to put them together after all. It seemed like they were two of a kind, neither of them with any ambition to be king of the block.

But Mad John was the unpredictable one of course, a murderous maniac who, like a cannibal spider, would destroy and gobble at will if the fancy took him. But it wasn't Clay Dachin who precipitated the shindig when, in recreation time, it burst upon the cell-block.

There was another character in the block, a life killer like Dachin who thought himself a hell of a feller and was wont to mutter threats against the gunfighter behind his back. Now he began to mutter about the 'big madman' whom he referred to also as 'that fancy gunny's friend'.

Dachin seemed oblivious to such spite. But Mad John Mulooney wasn't. He caught hold of the mutterer one fine morning in the small yard set apart for the most dangerous prisoners and commenced to strangle him.

It was Dachin who pulled them apart. And the

giant John turned on his erstwhile 'friend'.

It was a legendary fight, a fight to talk about for ever more.

John transferred his huge paws from the mutterer's throat to the throat of Dachin and began to squeeze, now making a guttural sound in his throat like some animal.

'He should've had his chopper,' some wag said.

But at first it didn't seem as if he needed it.

He was forcing Dachin downwards to the hard, beaten ground and the tall, lean man seemed to be choking. The fellow who had caused the battle to start stood apart, one hand clutched at his throat, his eyes bulging.

Dachin wore soft moccasins. He couldn't use his feet, wouldn't have done much harm with them if he had. He used one knee, driving it upwards viciously into John's groin. John's gutturals changed to an explosive bellowing grunt and his grip slackened and Dachin used both his arms in a scissors motion, his fists driving John's hands away from his throat.

Dachin lowered both fists then. He hit John two rapid blows in the gut: the giant was some adipose there. The man doubled, his wind rushing from his open mouth. Dachin brought his knee up and it cracked powerfully against John's now underslung jaw. He was propelled upwards and backwards all at the same time. Dachin hit him again; same place, same jaw, followed him catlike as he floundered, arms waving, but did not fall.

Attendant warders had been taken by surprise as

the action started. They even watched in amazement for a short time. Then they moved in, clubs swinging.

Dachin received a blow on the back of his head and fell against Mad John, forcing him the rest of the way to the ground in an embrace as if they were bosom friends. But the giant's hands were suddenly claws again. He was beaten unconscious and his fingers had to be prised from Dachin's throat as the lean man, spluttering, regained consciousness.

The still bulk of the giant mass murderer was carried to his cell.

Clay Dachin could walk now. He was marched to the place they called 'the hole', a term used in many jails of this kind, unimaginative, but the reality of it being none the less horrible.

In truth, though most of the guards, noted for more muscle than imagination, referred to the black punishment area as 'the hole' in the prevalent jail-like way, many of the convicts (and their copyists) with more brilliant, if twisted minds, had another name for it.

They called it The Pit.

It was the cellars of the grey, forbidding complex and consisted of four cells in a line with a narrow passage running in front of their doors, and two more doors, one at each end.

The cells had no windows, just small ventilators high in the ceilings. The cell doors were of immensely thick timber banded and studded with iron and had a single trap, low down, in each, which could only be opened from the outside. When this trap was closed, as it mostly was, a man could scream

19

his head off and nobody would hear him, didn't want to hear him.

Through these traps were quickly passed the bread and water which, for the duration of their stay in this deep incarceration, this tomb, was designed to keep the fractious wrongdoers alive.

Bread and water twice a day and, with that, only silence and darkness, *blackness*, not even small noises from around or above, only silence and the blackness.

A man could look upwards at the ventilator till his eyes ache and he might see a smidgen of light like a mockery.

This was a living death for whatever length of time seemed necessary to break a man's spirit, or rob him completely of his sanity.

There was a wooden bucket, often leaking, in the corner of each cell and in another corner a pile of rough blankets which was the man's bed, his seat, his everything: he had no table or bench or bunk.

The buckets were emptied by the prisoners during one short break period once a day. This was taken, each man by himself, at intervals in a small lobby-cum-washroom beyond one door off the passage. A man was allowed to wash there if he was quick about it.

There were always three guards in attendance who, with their charge, filled the small area. Clubs were ready. Intimidation and abuse was the watch-word.

The outer door from the washroom was as stout as its fellows and, like them, was securely locked and bolted on the outside. Not even the guards could get out until they gave the signals: three raps on their side with a stout knobbly club.

One guard invariably carried a specially modified sawn-off. It didn't take up much room. It would be hard for a prisoner to grab. One had tried, had been shot in the belly, had died in agony.

Nobody had ever escaped from The Pit. The Cap'n said that nobody ever would. The Cap'n thought he was infallible. *But nobody ever was* – the mischievous Fates saw to that.

THREE

Clay Dachin knew that he had to get out of Stark City as soon as possible, though right now nothing seemed at all likely. He hadn't planned to get himself banged-up in The Pit. But he wasn't disheartened: such a word wasn't part of his vocabulary.

He began to wonder if being in The Pit might even have given him a new angle.

A strange and desperate thought. But strange and desperate things had been part of his way of life for more years than he cared to remember.

He knew that he had friends (if he could call them that) who would want him out of here, would even try to get him out if they saw any chance.

He was, you might say, the crux, even the catalyst. But if he had told them that in so many words, they wouldn't have understood what he was talking about.

Jigger and Peaboy for instance. He thought of them first.

He did not know that Lady Luck was about to smile on him and that the two partners would get a smidgen of her favour also, though they'd have to work for it.

First they must travel to the border hellhole named Caliero, the place some folks (including Peaboy) called Hell's Back Door. Then they must find Panama Jack, set-up man, go-between, murder-broker, the one Jigger had called 'skelington'. And they must enlist his aid. For a price. Or the cut of some proceeds, whatever those proceeds might be.

Jigger and Peaboy were two of a kind. If Panama Jack double-crossed them he could lose his skull-head forever.

They found him. They faced him across a battered desk in the back room of a rathskellar in Caliero. He knew why they were there.

'I heard about Dachin,' he said.

'We've got somep'n lined up,' Peaboy said.

'I heard you were runnin' with that big ape Bruke,' said Jack. 'Where is he now?'

'He's watching our backs,' Jigger said.

'Does Dachin know you're using him?'

'He will.'

'This job?'

'We want a man to go in first, coast the lay of the land for us.'

'I have such a man.'

They were interrupted then by the door crashing open and a man hurtling in, the big form of the aforesaid Bruke right behind him, a little feller, Bruke towering over him.

'He's the man,' Panama Jack said.

'He was watching,' Bruke said.

There was a chance for explosive action, but nobody had shown a weapon yet.

'He's the one who watches my back,' Jack said. 'He's also the one who'll serve your purpose.'

'He ain't very big, is he?' said Jigger.

'He's fast. And he's very intelligent,' said Jack.

He didn't look either of those things, the little man : he was plump and pop-eyed and gazed from one to the other of them as if he didn't know what was going on.

He wore two guns, however, one in a low-slung holster, the other in the front of his belt.

Panama Jack rose to his feet. He looked like a grinning scarecrow.

'This is Billy Sarmo, boys,' he said.

Billy's plump face split in a grin. With his small white teeth he looked like a cherub. He held out his right hand, and Bruke had come abreast of him by then and it looked as if Billy wanted to shake hands with the big man, forgive him for his roughness.

But then, as the right hand remained lifted, the bovine Bruke not being quick enough to grasp it, Billy's left had dipped.

Next moment the gun was out of the front of his belt and gripped in his pudgy fist.

He backed. He covered them all.

'Goda'mighty,' said Peaboy.

'Put it away, Billy,' Panama Jack said. 'The boys are convinced. Aren't you, boys?'

'I dunno,' growled Jigger who was no bigger than Billy, though leaner, looked faster but wasn't.

'Hell, we're impressed,' said Peaboy.

24

Bruke, as usual, said nothing. Not until there were no weapons in argumentative view and they were all seated in a rough semi-circle did Bruke put in his two cents' worth.

He looked at Billy Sarmo and grinned a snaggle-toothed grin and said, 'He's quite a pippin, ain't he?'

It looked as if those two were gonna be friends after all.

The two boys hadn't had to ask Panama Jack to actually set up a job for them after all and were mighty glad of that. Jack always wanted to grab too much of the profit.

They had other connections and had looked in on some of them as they, with big Bruke in tow, had made their way to Hell's Back Door.

One of the connections had paid off. But now the boys had to work fast, the time of the job calling for that. So they didn't mind too much using Jack's services, including Billy Sarmo.

They also needed a powder-man, for they had some blowing to do.

Panama Jack found them a tough elderly cuss named Culey who had worked in mines and knew powder well.

Five men in all. That was figured enough. More would cost more.

Jigger said, 'We oughta take that damn' skelington along with us. He could light the fuse or somep'n.'

Old Culey said sternly, 'No man does any o' my job for me.'

Peaboy said, 'Let's get goin' then – we ain't get a lotta time.'

Neither Bruke or Sarmo said anything. They all rode. They had just enough time, toting a mule with the supplies they needed.

FOUR

At the last minute, on Panama Jack's advice, the boys recruited a second oldster – a colleague of powder-man Culey's but not a smart one – merely to hold the horses.

He was sent ahead to a grove of trees beside the rail-lines. This spot was about a mile from the rising bend where the iron horse invariably had to slow down.

There was a convenient outcrop of rocks over-looking the bend and here the rest of the band crouched.

Jigger, Peaboy, Billy Sarmo, Culey and Bruke.

The snake-like train was just crawling when they all jumped on at intervals, Bruke and Culey last, with the big man helping the powder-man with his gear.

The first three, Jigger, Peaboy and Billy had picked their places well. Jigger and Peaboy first, Billy not far behind them. And Peaboy had the despatch car picked well. He hammered on the door and called cheerfully, 'Comin' through.'

A porter, the folks inside must have thought. They

might have been a mite puzzled, even a mite wary, but the cheerful voice fooled them.

There was only two of them behind the barred door: the robbers had been assured of that and their informant – to be paid later – had been right.

One of the two bullion guards, gun in hand, opened the door a little and peered out.

Peaboy, the most muscular of the three attackers, charged the door violently. He didn't look cheerful. He had a gun in his fist and, as the guard staggered backwards, slashed him across the temple with the steel barrel.

The door was wide and Jigger whipped around the corner like a greased eel. He covered the second man with levelled pistol. 'Drop it,' he snarled.

The stupefied man hadn't even got it above waist-level. He dropped it. His partner was unconscious on the floor, blood running down the side of his face. The second man was told to lie down on his belly next to his mate and he did so. Jigger lashed his hands and his mate's hands behind them. The latter was coming-to, groaning.

The robbers' informant had only been partly right after all.

Two guards, yes. But also the usual despatch man, a sort of porter who always rode this carriage when it was needed; he was needed. He had been asleep in his tiny cubbyhole in the corner of the big strong-room-cum-carriage. He came out, blinking his eyes. A heavy sleeper, not yet fully awake, he opened his mouth wide, a yawn, a question.

Half-a-question: hardly a question at all. 'Wha—?'

'Shut it,' snarled Jigger. 'Get down there.'

The man lay on his belly beside the other two and had his wrists trussed.

'Not a sound, y'hear?' Jigger said. 'Understand.' And at that moment Billy Sarmo was coming through the door. The prisoners understood. They were but paid employees and they knew desperate men when they were confronted by them bristling with hardware. They didn't aim to stick their necks out.

The pistol-whipped man murmured some kind of assent. His partner made no sound at all, didn't move. The elderly despatch man seemed to be dozing off again.

Bruke and Culey came through the door and, turning, Peaboy asked, 'Anything movin' back there?'

'Doesn't look like it,' said Bruke.

Culey was already making a beeline for the strongbox in the corner.

Peaboy looked at Billy Sarmo, said, 'Stand watch outside.'

'Right, chief,' said Billy, dimpling like a cherub.

'Don't shoot anybody if you don't have to,' added Peaboy sardonically.

'I never waste bullets,' said Billy, and then he was out of sight.

Turning away from the strongbox where he was setting a fuse, Culey said. 'We've gotta get out of here till it blows. You don't want these three blown to Kingdom Come, do you?'

They thought this would be pretty unnecessary. Having negotiated the bend, the train picking up speed, the prisoners, their hands still tied were shoved out into the corridor. Culey laid a thin trail of powder.

The bunch burst into the nearest carriage which was partially full of people, who all turned to stare. They were alarmed by the sight of three men, hands behind their backs, one of them with blood still running sluggishly down his white face.

They were menaced by men with drawn guns which seemed to put a clincher on things, to say the least.

'Up with the hands,' snapped the little dark man with the mean face. A taller man at his side turned to another small feller, plump, boyish-looking, said, 'Go an' stop it. We haven't got much time.'

The cherubic little man moved fast. As the bullion coach had been cunningly placed in the middle of the train, he didn't have far to go.

He must have done what had been planned. The train began to slow.

There was a small forest of uplifted hands. The passengers looked to be a harmless, frightened bunch.

Culey bent, scratched a lucifer, set it to the powder trail, started it spluttering.

'There's gonna be an explosion!' Peaboy yelled. 'Get down below your seats, all o' you.'

There was a frenzied scramble. Heads disappeared. The robbers crouched down too, but they kept their guns at the ready.

The train had come to a grinding halt.

The explosion shook the carriage. Amid the

echoes, a woman screamed. Timber crashed. Dust and debris fell. But in the carriage there was no great damage and nobody was hurt.

Carrying gunny sacks, Bruke went back with Culey.

Jigger was peering out of the window. 'We're right there,' he said.

The big man and the elderly powder-man returned with bulging gunny sacks.

'It was good,' said Bruke.

'I tol' yuh,' said Culey.

They left the crouching passengers, the two guards and the despatch man still crouching down and they all went through towards where Billy, his gun at the backs of the driver and the engineer, awaited them.

Jigger called back, 'Anybody gets up or tries any funny business it'll be the worse for 'em, I promise you.'

He didn't look or sound as vicious as his small, dark companion who maybe had some Injun in him, but his steady, deep voice carried menacing conviction.

A few moments later all the robbers were jumping the train, making for the grove of trees just off the side of the shining steel rails.

They were at the edge of the trees and could see Culey's friend and the horses when the unforeseen happened.

From back in the train a gun boomed, the sound coming from the front part which was in direct line to the escaping outlaws.

Culey gave a small, choked cry and pitched forward, losing hold of the gunny sacks. Bruke, also

31

carrying sacks, dropped on one knee beside Culey, laid his sack down, drew his gun, raised it. But the train windows at the point opposite were empty. Whoever had fired the gun had ducked out of sight, maybe alarmed that they had hit somebody after all.

This was a chance that the boys had had to take; and taken. A small army would have had to be employed to override something like this and such a force would have been impractical – and costly.

'He's dead,' said Bruke. 'Right in the back of the head.'

'Leave him,' yelled Peaboy. 'Grab those bags an' get in here.'

There was no more shooting. Bruke made it into the trees, sacks and all.

The elderly horse-holder who had been Culey's friend made as if to go out there but Jigger forestalled the move.

Peaboy said, 'Don't be loco. That shootin' fool back there might try another potshot. You can't do anything to help Culey now. We've gotta move.'

They moved fast, set their horses at a gallop, made it out of the trees on the other side, losing sight of the train.

'Good huntin',' yelled Billy Sarmo. 'Mighty good huntin'!'

He laughed like a crazy boy.

FIVE

Panama Jack had a surprise for the boys, something he had been keeping up his sleeve till they got back. If they got back! He said he was very sorry to hear about the death of old Culey, but that was the chance an old owlhoot bird like Culey had to take, that all of them had to take.

Peaboy asked scornfully what he, Jack, figured were the chances he took, sitting on his bony ass waiting for the boodle to roll in?

The takings from the train hadn't been as good as expected, Peaboy now divulged, not as good as their informant had reckoned – and they'd had to pay him off too.

They figured, though, that they had enough, after giving Jack his cut (Jack had ignored the jibe) to hire a few more men for the job on Stark City.

Jack, his teeth grinning in his skull face, said he had something else in hand, for another consideration of course.

'Consideration' seemed to be his favourite word.

'For Chris'sakes,' said Jigger. 'Let's be hearing it then.'

Jack said there was right here in Caliero a feller, a friend of his in fact, who had recently come out after a spell in Stark City.

The boys were introduced to a quick-talking confidence trickster who had been attacked by one of his victims with a knife. In the ensuing mêlée the victim had also been cut badly, and had survived. But the trickster who went by the moniker of Kelley Rodd hadn't been able to talk his way out of this one. He had been indicted, sentenced. He said that Stark City was a living hell and he'd surely help anybody who wanted to be out of there.

The boys went along. Maybe they figured that Rodd might be able to trick his way into Stark City and out again – with Clay Dachin and all. Rodd, a smart jasper in broadcloth and sporting a flowing moustache, had a small paunch and shrewd and twinkling eyes.

Billy Sarmo volunteered to come along – at Jack's sayso. The boys accepted him. They said they figured on two more, making seven in all, as the deceased Culey's horse-toting colleague wasn't volunteering it seemed. Less mightn't be enough, more too many: they'd probably have to split anyway.

Panama Jack introduced Peaboy, Jigger and Bruke to two hard-faced young gunnies called briefly Dan and Sep. Meanwhile Kelley Rodd was making a map of all he remembered of Stark City.

He said he knew the trail across the badlands pretty well and, although this wasn't his usual type of undertaking, he'd be the guide.

Dan and Sep exchanged glances, and one of them said he and his partner knew the badlands kinda genuinely also, had used the various trails now and then. But they'd have to take plenty of vittles and, most of all, well-filled canteens.

They all poured over Rodd's map. Dan and Sep, who didn't take very much to this smart-talking dude, voiced their reluctant approval. They were ready; Panama Jack wished them well; Peaboy laughed derisively; they left Hell's Back Door.

Clay Dachin was in the washroom adjacent to The Pit. There were two guards in attendance, one with a sawn-off shotgun. The door leading right out of that section and away from The Pit was tightly closed, looked ominously heavy, completely impregnable.

The knocking on its barred and iron-studded wood was sudden and thunderous.

It was the signal, though, three knocks. 'Who in hell's that?' said the guard with the bamboo club, a six-shooter in his belt. 'They shouldn't be here right now, not yet.'

'Do it anyway,' said the guard with the shotgun and he backed off a little, covering the prisoner, warily, a cruel, sardonic light in the piggy eyes.

Dachin gave him a thin smile which didn't reach the cold eyes in the set, handsome face. Dachin knew that this kind of silent insolence irritated these bully-boys. He then pretended to ignore both guards completely. But his mind raced.

One of the cells back in The Pit was unoccupied,

its late occupant having been taken to the sick bay – if you could call it that – and had subsequently handed in his pail, another candidate for the badlands burial ground.

Out of the corner of his eye, Dachin watched the big door.

He watched the door open and the guard stand back from it, but then look startled, raising his club. A giant of a man came rapidly through the gap, his shoulder pushing the door wider.

Mad John Mulooney, obviously better now from his hurts and condemned to join his erstwhile sparring partner, Clay Dachin, in The Pit.

There were two guards with Mulooney.

He saw Dachin, and he bellowed with rage and started for him, taking everybody by surprise, including Dachin. In sending the loco giant through at this time somebody had made an error of judgement.

And the outcome was a lightning, explosive fragment of hell.

The guard with the shotgun was faster than he looked. Gun lifted, he moved in front of Mad John and barked, 'Stay', as if he were talking to a fractious hound.

The giant made a guttural animal sound, raised a clublike fist and brought it down very hard on the top of the guard's bare head which was bulletlike and almost bald.

The man groaned and wilted. But his finger must have contracted on the trigger of the shotgun and it went off, the sound hideous in the enclosed space.

John caught the charge full in the belly and it

almost blew him half. Then he and the unconscious guard were in a tangled pile on the floor. The shotgun skidded along the floor which was wet in places, and Clay Dachin bent and grabbed it. He had been the wary one and his wariness had paid off.

One barrel of the gun was unfired. The three remaining guards had been overwhelmed by a shocked surprise, the bloody carnage – they weren't quick enough to get their guns. Also the stunned guard's partner was near to the prisoner who took another advantage, reached out and plucked the man's Colt from its holster.

He rested the shotgun on his hip and backed so that he could cover all three men completely with the sawn-down long gun and the long-barrelled pistol.

He made a gesture. 'Over there in the corner,' he said. He glared at the two newcomers. 'Take off your hardware an' drop it on the floor, then kick it over here.'

'You can't—'

'Do as I say!' His strange cold eyes spelled murder. The three guards did what he'd told them to do and also complied with his next command. He wanted their keys. He got them.

He unlocked the inner door which led into The Pit and shepherded the three men into the narrow passage. He propped the shotgun against the wall where none of them could reach it. Then, covering them with two Colts, one of which he had stashed in his belt after picking it up in the washroom, he unlocked the two cell-doors and let out the occupants.

They were both men of about his own age and he had learned that their names were Dulus and Quane. He jerked his head, said, 'There are two more guns back there. Take 'em. We're goin' out of here. But you do as I say, y'understand?'

'We will,' said Dulus.

Quane, a silent brooder with one lazy eye merely nodded his head.

'We're goin' as quietly as we can,' Dachin told them. 'No shootin' 'less it's unavoidable. You're goin' in front o' me but at my guidance. I'll shoot either of you who tries anything funny.'

'Right,' said Dulus. 'Let's get goin' then.'

They locked the three guards in the cells, locked the passage door behind them, went through the washroom where Dulus and Quane collected a gun apiece. The outer door yawned. But there was a lot of tortuous and perilous territory ahead of them yet. Two men lay in blood.

'Goda'mighty, Clay,' said Dulus. 'Did you do that?'

'Not entirely.' Dachin hadn't given Dulus permission to call him Clay. Still, maybe he had a good ally there. Dulus had a grim, angular face but steady eyes.

'It's Mad John,' said Quane, and his lazy eye didn't blink.

The giant was very obviously dead. But the unconscious guard began to groan and struggle from under the bloody hulk that held him.

'Drag him through an' put him in the empty cell,' said Dachin, handing over the keys.

Quane took them, said, 'Should cut the throats of the three of 'em.'

'Do as I say.' Dachin's voice was suddenly a snarl and his eyes were like burning ice.

'C'mon,' said Dulus. 'We ain't got time for any argument, Rafe.'

Dachin hadn't known that Quane's first name was Rafe. I might have to leave that jasper behind after all, he thought, fleetingly.

They might all get left behind, dead meat for the burial grounds.

The two men returned, closed the communicating door.

The trio, with Dachin in the lead, went through the outer wash-house door, slamming it behind them.

They knew there was another door ahead of them, a lobby, two more armed guards. If they got through there they still had to negotiate grey territory that none of them knew very well, a perilous journey indeed.

Now, unspeaking, Quane and Dulus seemed to be following Dachin's lead.

SIX

There was another stout, thick, iron-fortified door in front of them. No more guards: they were obviously on the other side. The three prisoners came to an abrupt halt and obscenities were exchanged when Dachin discovered that, on the two huge key-rings he had, there was no key for this door.

There was a keyhole. But it seemed very new this side, was perhaps virtually unused.

Dachin said, 'Maybe they just knock.' He jerked his head. 'Like they did back there. I'm gonna try it.'

Rafe Quane began, 'What—'

Dachin knocked three times on the door with the butt of a captured Colt. 'Spread out,' he said. There was just room to do that.

But the door was opened towards them, causing Quane and Dulus to draw even further back behind Dachin.

Dachin pulled the door wider.

There was a guard there. He had a gun in his belt, but all there was in his hand appeared to be the inevitable bambooo club. A formidable weapon but

40

no match for the gun Dachin pointed at the man's gut, fingerlike, close enough to blow a hole right through him.

With his free hand, Dachin snatched the club from the man's grip before, in his surprise, he could drop it with a clatter to the hard floor.

He jerked the gun and the wide-eyed guard backed and then Dachin moved aside to let his two fellow-escapees through. Quane hit the man across the temple with a gun-barrel and Dulus caught him and lowered him to the floor. These two were working together well now. Their leader could only hope that they continued that way. But things were fraught now as another guard appeared from the door of what appeared to be a small kitchen in back of this office-cum-strongroom. Stark City was like a sprawling conglomeration of strongrooms of various sizes and vulnerabilties, but which were in the main savagely impregnable.

The second guard was no idiot. He raised his hands before a trio of levelled guns and Quane pistol-whipped him into unconsciousness. He didn't need catching by Dulus, hit the floor with a soft thud: there was nothing behind him but another door.

This was not as stout as those that had gone before it. To the three prisoners' surprise it was found to be unlocked and, in single file, with Dachin still in the lead, they went through it.

There was a long grey passage, and nobody in sight. It was a narrow outlet, the men still having to pace in single file, but they moved more speedily than before.

They had to move as swiftly as possible, keep moving. Quane had wanted to slit throats. . . . But he seemed to have gotten rid of that idea. He even grinned as they hit the air which was like a breath of new life.

These men were outdoor men.

But they hadn't had time to plan. Dachin had seen a chance, grabbed it. It had been ironical that his late sparring partner Mad John Mulooney had, indirectly, been the crazy instigator of that plan. It was a pity, Dachin thought sardonically, that Mad John hadn't been able to come along also: he might've been an asset.

They moved along a wall in a small sort of exercise yard that none of them had seen before – and there was not another soul in sight.

There was a narrow gate which was unlocked and they passed though it, one by one, with great wariness. Quane was still grinning, though that didn't do much for his funny eyes. Dulus was chuckling like a kid playing hookey.

'Take it easy,' Dachin said. 'And no shootin', or we might bring the whole damn' place about our heads.'

His two companions became solemn-faced again, nodded their heads.

Dachin had another of his fleeting thoughts. This end of the sprawling jail didn't seem to have much security at all. Did the Cap'n think that his fortress was so impregnable that only the main places where commerce came and went, where prisoners were brought in or released, was the only area that needed the big watch?

High grey walls were all around the three lone men and now there didn't seem to be a break of any kind, no door, no gap.

Maybe the Cap'n had the rights of it after all! Dachin had wanted a plan. Given time he would've had a plan, in The Pit, or out of it. But he'd seen his chance and he'd taken it. He asked himself, what else could I have done? Hell, Mad John might've killed him, and those guards also. Dachin had never met anybody quite like John before and now he kind of missed him.

They went around the walls like cats. And then Dachin, who was still a little ahead of the other two, spotted the wooden, iron-studded trap in the hard flat ground. He got down on one knee so abruptly that Dulus almost fell over him.

The trio clustered. There was a big iron ring set into the trap. Dachin grabbed it, lifted it. He yanked hard, grunting. The trap began to lift.

It came right up. They looked down into a gaping hole.

It was daylight still and the air was fresh. To them it had been like wine and the pale sun had made them blink. But now the sun was going down, a redness like blood.

Their shadows filled the hole. But Dachin drew aside and the red sun and the darkening skies gave them enough light to see into the yawning pit and the flight of steps that went down into blackness that no light seemed able to penetrate.

'We've gotta go down there,' Dachin said.

From one Pit to another.

But they followed him down the steps, and the last man, who happened to be Dulus, closed the trap behind them, shutting them in absolute darkness, a blackness even deeper than that they had known in their cells in The Pit, *the real pit*.

Dachin hit bottom. Goddamn, he thought, I should have grabbed some lucifers from the guards.

But the plan had been to break out – or die trying – not to return to another pit.

Dachin had stashed his gun. He used his hands. He could feel Quane close behind him. He felt around each side of the two of them, knowing Dulus was close behind Quane, maybe still on the bottom step.

Dachin had counted the steps. Fourteen of them. They were down pretty deep. He felt a hard, slimy wall to the left of him but nothing to the right. He told the boys to turn that way and follow him. His voice echoed in a ghostly way.

Their footsteps echoed. It was as if they were in a tomb. The air got damp. Their passage was narrow and the walls were slimy. Then they heard water dripping and Dachin said he'd felt something like pipes.

'Yeh,' said Dulus who was still last in line. 'Where the hell are we?'

There was near-panic in his voice.

SEVEN

Dachin was thinking straighter, and remembering. He suddenly half-realized where they were.

He hoped he was right – like hell!

One way or another, however, there was still plenty of gut-grinding hell ahead of them. Stark City was not just a big hoosegow, it was a sprawling penal settlement.

Apart from the fact that it was named after a megalomaniac of the same title, though usually called derisively 'the Cap'n', it was in a stark, waterless area and that fitted the name also. Escapees – and there hadn't been many – had died horribly from thirst out in the wastelands.

Water had to be brought to the main compound by tanks on covered wagons in the same way as other supplies. Dachin had heard that most of the supplies, including the water, came from a sweet creek and an outlaw town called Caliero, which was also known as Hell's Back Door, this being not far from the borderlands and the big river.

When in the main area, before he was incarcerated in The Pit, Dachin had once seen the water carts, as they were called, come into the compound. The precious liquid was jettisoned into huge tanks sunk in the ground which were covered afterwards with stout round trapdoors, barred and padlocked.

A half-crazy man had once tried to escape by jumping into one of the pools after evading the guards. He had been shot in the back many times and had sunk like a rock. The body had never been recovered and, for a while after that, the old lags referred to the water-supply as 'dead man's drink'.

The water was drawn up, Dachin had been told, by an elaborate form of suction and pipes which supplied hand pumps and small wells in strategic places.

Dachin remembered something else he had heard. It was said that Stark City was on the site of an old burial ground, a succession of tombs built by the ancient Pueblo Indians who had thrived in the borderlands centuries ago.

But was this just another legend that had grown up about such a place? Not much was known about those ancient people anyway, Dachin thought. Perhaps their enemies the old Spaniards had built a fortress.

The prison's actual burial ground was outside its perimeter, everybody knew that.

But what if the settlement had been built *over* an ancient burial ground after all, and the pits used for the drainage and a primitive water system, once filled with outside supplies, could keep that harsh penal establishment afloat in more ways than one?

Thoughts to conjure with.

And then Quane, peering over Dachin's shoulder, said, almost with excitement, 'I see glimmers of light ahead.'

'Take it carefully,' said Dachin, also spotting the meagre light which seemed to be filtering in from above.

He slowed down and Quane followed suit. Dulus butted into Quane and said, 'God, I'd like to be out of here.'

Dachin wondered, how did that man stand all that time in The Pit? Dulus sounded desperate. But maybe some desperation was needed as planning had been so scant.

'I think we've got more than a chance, my friends,' Dachin said.

Friends? Enigmatic, unpredictable unknowns!

Slivers of light through cracks, the source yet unknown, sending thin pencils down to glimmer on steel. Rounded edges and things that looked like pipes. . . .

It was like Dachin's half-imagined theories, the pictures in his mind come true. 'The tanks,' he whispered. But how to get above them, how to reach the hatches, barred, bolted, seemingly impregnable. Were they any better off than they'd been before, Dachin and his 'friends', or were they trapped, having exchanged one pit for yet another?

Panama Jack had more news for the boys. A supply train was due to leave Caliero for Stark City.

It would be heavily guarded and the sharpshooters

and their Mexican comrades would be mighty wary of any strangers who came near, might even shoot a few strangers out of hand.

But there were, of course, other ways of leaving town.

The boys were all ready. Peaboy, Jigger, Bruke, Billy Sarmo. And the two young, hard new fish called Dan and Sep. And then there was the ex-convict who had served a stretch in the penal settlement, was named Kelley Rodd and would be there to guide. Rodd, ex-confidence trickster with his small paunch and flowing moustache.

He said, oh, yes, he knew other trails. The supply train would take the straight route. He knew others. How many guards would there be, Peaboy asked? Usually about six, Rodd said, and Panama Jack and Billy Sarmo agreed with this.

'We could take 'em,' Billy said. 'We put the gunnies down – and the muleskinners, particularly the low-paid peons, ain't gonna stick their jibs out far.'

'We'll work that out later,' Peaboy said.

They watched, from Jack's place, the supply train leave town. Then they set out themselves, armed to the ears and with plenty of supplies themselves to give them sustenance, everything strapped to the horses: pack mules would have slowed them down.

'Somebody might've given an alarm by now,' said Dulus.

'We'd hear the bell if they rang it, I think,' said Dachin.

Their eyes were getting more accustomed to the woolly darkness lit here and there by slivers of light. A small wait, that was Dachin's plan. Then he pointed upwards. 'Pipes up there,' he said. 'I think I can climb them. Give me a lift.'

Dulus helped him to hoist himself on to Quane's shoulders. Steel was wet and slimy to his touch. He scrabbled, slipped. Quane swayed. Dulus held him.

Dachin reached upwards until he felt his arm was coming out of its socket. His shoulders and neck throbbed with strain.

His clutching fingers found purchase on an angle of pipe. There was a smooth sliminess. Water dripped on his face.

'At least we can get a drink,' he gasped. Hell, he should've planned better than this. They hadn't come at all well-prepared, hadn't even known what was ahead of them. And this, so far, was it.

His fingers slipped, came away. He uttered a smothered curse as he felt himself falling. He cursed his helplessness. And then he was in a tangle on the hard floor with his two companions.

They sorted themselves out. Dulus, who had been underneath, was gasping for breath. Dachin could see the whites of his eyes.

'That was only the first try,' Dachin said. 'C'mon.'

They tried again. No more words. Saving their energy, using it, gasping, straining.

Dachin tried another hold. He made it. He was wringing wet, and some of that was sweat: he could smell it. He could smell metal too. He could smell water. He hadn't realized that water could smell. He told himself it was a good smell.

The smells assailed him, good or bad. Should've had steps or a ladder down here, he thought, so that those stupid bastards up top could get down here in an emergency.

But, of course, they could lower something down here, couldn't they? A rope ladder for instance. He thought of dead bodies floating. He hauled himself upwards desperately. He was away from the other two now, did not look down.

He was wet. He ached all over. He needed a rest but figured that if he stopped, hell, he might stop for good, would maybe be back in The Pit then where he could rest. What are you doing, he asked himself, what are you thinking, are you going damn' loco?

He gritted his teeth and grunted through them and he stretched and hauled and almost cried out with the pain. To cry out would be a relief. But down below Dulus and Quane were silent. He knew they were looking up, staring. Could they still see him?

He had a terrible feeling that he might fall again. God, how he wanted to stop for a bit! But he didn't.

How much further . . . *how much?*

EIGHT

What had he been thinking? Hell, the guards could get into this underground place by the same way the three escapees had used. The guards could bring ladders or, in a real emergency, maybe some kind of climbing gear.

If the escape alarm had been given they could be planning something already. Maybe they'd already figured how the prisoners had managed to go missing, to disappear. The Cap'n himself could've figured that.

If the guards were already moving in the same way, they could find Dachin and his two colleagues down here. We'll be trapped, Dachin thought.

All right, they all had guns and they could use them. Dachin had no illusions about Dulus and Quane. They were killers. Not maybe as professional a *pistolero* as Dachin was himself. No, he thought sardonically, but they would fight like cornered rats.

He, and they, would give a mighty strong account of themselves.

But what the outcome eventually would be didn't

bear thinking about.

He stopped thinking about what might happen and concentrated on the here and now.

Above him was wood, stout in the ghostly, barely lit woolly darkness. He raised one hand, pressed against the hard surface, steadying himself.

He was on the edge of one of the water tanks. The rim of it took his other hand. Blessed rest!

He turned his head slowly and looked down. He could see no figures clearly, only sort of sense them. But he knew they were there. There was no sound from them.

Maybe they'd been thinking the way he'd been thinking, examining in their minds the seeming hopelessness of their position.

Great Jehosophat, thought Dachin, how am I gonna get 'em up outa here?

There was something that Panama Jack had forgotten to mention to the boys. Or maybe he hadn't thought of it as important enough. The water carts carrying the precious fluid that was so necessary for the well-being of Stark City usually started out on the same day as the other supply wagons but somewhat earlier.

They didn't have a bunch of armed guards as did the supply folks, paid for by the local businessmen, crooked jaspers all, who now made a mighty good thing out of selling goods and necessities to the big Pen.

But, hell, who'd stick up water carts anyway? There was plenty of water back in town and a sweet water creek nearby and the big river not far. Who'd want to steal water?

Jack, comfortable and safe in his billet, had expected the boys to ride fast, knowing that they would have to make a detour. The hired ones would be paid well for their job. Billy Sarmo and his colleagues, Dan and Sep, were young and reckless and completely amoral.

Kelley Rodd was a different mess of fish altogether. Intelligent, venal, sardonic, a man who loved money and wanted revenge for having to pay for his sins by a stretch in Stark City.

The three young hardcases were in the caper for the hell of it as well as the money. They didn't care whether the prison settlement and its watchers suffered or not. They didn't even know Clay Dachin, though they'd heard of him.

So Peaboy, Jigger and Bruke were actually the collective driving force behind this seemingly reckless caper, with the giant Bruke, strangely, the most anxious. He followed Peaboy's lead, however – and even the snakelike Jigger did that now. And Peaboy led them, fast and uncompromising, for that was the way he was.

And, with the co-operation of the locals, Billy, Dan and Sep, Kelley Rodd was their guide.

Having galloped over hard, bare ground and coming towards the straight, though hardly discernicble, trail at an angle, they saw the water carts. Billy Sarmo identified them for what they were.

Peaboy thought fast. Then he said, 'We'll take 'em.'

'That'd be easier than taking the supply wagons,' Billy affirmed. 'That'll be behind some place.'

'Yeh, I figured we'd outpace them. Get out your guns.' Peaboy laughed. 'Wave 'em threateningly but don't use 'em 'less you have to.'

They went in fast, spreading out, circling like warlike Indians.

Dachin pushed again at the wooden trap. It merely creaked, a small sound barely discernible above the drip-drip and trickle of water, an incessant goad. But a goad that did little for the man – and his pards – who were desperate to escape from a hell-hole. And that was what this subterranean chamber had become, thought the man who had climbed, couldn't help feeling now that it had been all for nothing.

He could see the outside, see it in his mind. Remembering the stout bars and padlocks, the iron studs; remembering the way the peons who brought the water had had to strain to lift those heavy round doors as the guards stood watching, armed, grinning, and the pitiless sun beating down on it all.

Clay Dachin had been in tight corners before. Many of them. Starting when, as just a boy, he had been left hanging on a vigilante's rope, accused of a crime he hadn't committed. He had been saved by an outlaw uncle and his bunch.

And that was how it had all started. . . .

Since then maybe he had earned a rope. He had certainly earned jail-time, had never had any till now. And this was the be-all and end-all. The tightest of corners and no loophole, just tiny cracks that could not be widened except by dynamite. And all he and his friends had were pistols, puny by comparison.

54

A disembodied voice called him from below. Plaintive; was it the voice of Dulus?

The water washed; *whispered* in the tank the edges of which held Dachin. It was as if his climbing in its proximity had disturbed it in some way.

He looked down into it. It was as if something had compelled him to do so.

A bare skull, white even in the darkness, floating, grinned up at him in mockery. . . .

NINE

The raid on the water carts turned out to be somewhat of a damp squib, nothing like the noisy, sparkling fireworks that the Mexicans loved so much at fiesta time.

And most of these people were Mexicans standing mute. And Billy Sarmo calling, 'That you, Juan?'

'Eet is, Señor Billee.' This came from a rotund, wide-grinning Mexican with a big hat and a shotgun that he didn't attempt to raise.

There were two Anglos who, at first, had appeared more warlike, slung guns and all which they hadn't had time to pull. All pointing in their direction, firepower literally bristled. Young Dan went round behind them and collected their gear.

Peaboy and Bruke dismounted and made a pedestrian circle of the carts and their keeps and drivers and the small wagon that carried the tucker and water the company needed on their long, dry journey. There was heat, but the sun was turning red.

Moving the flap to one side on the small covered wagon, Peaboy got a surprise. There were two

Mexican *putas* in there and they both squealed. One of them was stark naked, olive and shadowy in the sun-striped gloom. The other was on the point of getting dressed, had one leg in her fancy pantaloons.

The two men with them were partially covered and sort of cowering, caught with their pants down, likely.

'So they bring their own entertainment,' Peaboy said over his shoulder to the goggling Bruke. He thrust his head forward again, jerked the gun in his hand and snarled, 'Make it quick. An' get down from there.'

The quartet presented themselves, the men quietly acquiescent, the girls coy, in a more respectable way. The two girls were greeted by Billy as Adelia and Rosa and, like fat Juan, now minus his shotgun, greeted him as 'Señor Billee.' Dan and Sep knew the girls too. Dan wanted to know whether they'd been running a chain and all he got in reply was a smattering of giggles. But the two nubile fillies weren't half bad at that.

'Have we got time, boss?' asked Dan's partner, Sep.

'No, we ain't got time,' snapped Peaboy.

At first it seemed the fun-loving boys might want to argue about this. But Peaboy's sidekick Jigger was at his shoulder now, looking as small, mean and dark as always. Bruke was adjacent also, still looking at the girls as if they were made of angel cake.

The two young hardcases drew in their horns, and Peaboy looked at the assembled company and said, 'We're taking over.'

There was a thud. One of the Anglo hardcases had drawn a sneak derringer from a hold-out place and

Kelley Rodd had slugged him with a long-barrelled Remington pistol, leaving him senseless on the sun-baked earth. His partner backed off, holding out empty hands while Rodd bent and picked up the little pistol, referring to it as a toy.

The ex-confidence trickster, though looking nothing like a gunfighter, was certainly making his presence felt.

'Tie those two up an' put 'em in the little wagon,' Peaboy said. 'Gag 'em too. Move!'

Bruke took his eyes off the girls at last, and he found his rope.

'Have the girls got spare horses?' Peaboy wanted to know.

Juan said spare mounts were available. The girls were put on these and didn't look amiss.

'They can ride behind the wagon outa sight,' went on Peaboy. 'Go with 'em, big feller. Watch 'em.'

Bruke, his man-roping task completed, began to goggle at the girls again. He followed them.

'Think we can trust 'im?' young Dan asked, caustically.

'We can trust him!' snapped Peaboy. He gestured. 'We want this bunch back o' the carts all together so they can be watched.'

'Juan will watch them,' said Billy Sarmo. 'Ain't that right, Juan? Panama Jack knows Juan. Panama Jack will look after Juan. Ain't that right, Juan?'

'That ees right, Señor Billee,' said the fat man, grinning, obsidian eyes twinkling in olive pouches.

The girls were giggling again; the men could hear them. Young Dan looked askance but didn't say anything.

'Let's get on with it.' Peaboy was getting very impatient now.

But then Billy Sarmo said something. 'Aren't we forgetting. . . ?'

'What?'

'The supply wagons won't be far behind. They have armed guards. No matter what we do even when we get to Stark City that bunch will be on our tails.'

'He's right,' said Kelley Rodd.

'I guess he is,' Peaboy admitted. 'We'll have to take 'em then.' He was effectively in command again, and his friend Jigger was grinning at him as if taking on a bunch of gunslingers was way up their alley. And, with a sort of fatalism, nobody argued.

The sun was low and red, and Kelley was pointing with a plump forefinger. 'There's a cluster of rocks over that way. I can just see 'em. They're the only real genuine rocks for miles. We could pretend an accident over there, a wheel hit a rock or something. Try and draw those gunnies off.'

'Let's get to it then,' said Peaboy.

'I'll help,' said fat Juan.

'How about the others?'

'They do as I say.'

'Jack'll appreciate this,' said Billy, and gave the Mexican muleskinner leader back his shotgun.

They set things up well. Juan's boys clustered around one cart, its wheel pushed against a rock shaped like a huge mutilated thumb. Peaboy and the rest backed to the smaller wagon and hid themselves after Peaboy told the fat man, 'If this works we'll take over. You boys take cover.'

'I'll help.' Juan was repeating himself. But he meant what he said.

'All right.'

They got set. Bruke was at the flap of the small wagon, the two girls near him, the two trussed gun-guards lying in the back of the equipage.

As they waited, Kelley Rodd, ex-convict, was telling Peaboy about the pits in the compound at Stark City, the great water tanks inside them, the stout locked and barred traps on top.

He went on, 'Sometimes the supply train caught the water carts up by the time they got to the prison gates.'

'That's interesting to know,' said Peaboy.

'They're comin',' said Billy Sarmo, who was crouching beside Juan and keeping watch. Billy and his *amigo* drew back: the fat Mexican and the plump but fast-moving young gunfighter seemed to understand each other very well.

They watched the supply train draw to a halt. The peons around the water carts began to look uneasy. 'Wait for the word, my friends,' said Juan, but not too loudly. They had already been told they must draw back when the gunfighting force came forward, And soon those jaspers were doing just that, led by a scrubbily bearded tall man.

'Joley Brigg,' said Billy, 'A fast gun. Watch 'im.'

Then Brigg called, 'What's goin' on?'

Juan showed himself then, the butt of his double-barrelled long gun on the ground. 'We hit a rock, got a busted wheel.'

There were four behind Brigg and they followed

him, bunching now as, half-bent, their leader peered, not quite close enough yet to see the way the wheel was against the thumb-shaped rock. He hadn't drawn a gun and neither had any of his boys.

Then Peaboy and his boys came into view, bristling with armour, all of it levelled, primed. 'Hold it,' said Peaboy. 'Up with your hands, all o' yuh.'

Brigg whirled on Juan, maybe planning to use him as a shield (the fat Mex was certainly big enough for that), starting to draw. But Juan elevated his shotgun and let off a barrel.

Brigg was driven backwards by the slug hitting him at close range. His legs kicked up and then the rest of him. His head hit the ground and he stretched out and lay still.

Hands went up. None of the late Brigg's friends were aiming to commit suicide.

Over at the supply train folks were staring. A man broke away on a horse and set off at a gallop to the penal settlement which couldn't be seen yet.

Peaboy yelled, 'He's out to give the alarm.'

Kelley Rodd drew a rifle from its saddle scabbard and raised it to his shoulder, moved it in a gentle swing, drew a bead, pressed the trigger. The horseman came out of his saddle as if he'd been hit by an invisible fist. The echoes of the rifle shot resounded, died. The man went over his horse's head in a nose-dive, hit the ground, lay still. The horse went on but then slowed down, turned, trotted back.

'That cayuse ain't aiming to give any alarm,' Jigger said.

'That was some shootin', Kelly, man,' said Peaboy.

'We'll go over, me an' Bruke,' said Jigger. 'Cover us. C'mon, big feller.'

Bruke followed obediently.

Kelley hadn't said anything, held his Winchester rifle slackly at his side as if he didn't know what to do with it any more, whether to put it back in its saddle scabbard or to throw it away.

'Really damn' fine shooting,' said Peaboy, as if to himself now, but still looking at the plump moustached, ex-con.

Kelley looked solemn, even sad. 'That was another of my capabilities,' he said. 'But I've never shot a man before.' He looked at his rifle as if he hated it, but then he turned and put it back in its place on his horse's saddle.

Peaboy, a seasoned professional with any kind of gun, and wizard with a knife, thought, however, he knew how Kelley Rodd felt. But Peaboy didn't say any more, was watching Jigger and Bruke. Dan and Sep were herding the captured gunslingers together and tying them with rawhide of which they seemed to have plenty.

'Hell, we ought to shoot you all an' bury you here,' said Dan to one of the pistol-men who was giving him chat. He sounded jocular but his eyes were nasty.

Weapons were being collected. 'Lay 'em down,' said Peaboy. 'And put a canteen by each of them.'

One of them shouted, 'Our hands tied, how're we gonna drink?'

'You'll manage. Wriggle. Crawl. Maybe we'll pick you up on the way back.' Soon they were like so many logs, canteens near their faces, Sep's bright idea: they could use their teeth he said.

Jigger and Bruke were having no trouble. The horseman who had been shot had evidently been the only gunfighter left behind when his comrades visited the motionless water carts.

There were two bodies. In separate places. But not far apart. They would have to be left.

'Let's join the train,' said Peaboy to Juan and the fat man gave the order and the carts began to roll.

Unwieldy. Wobbling. Wide barrels on the flat beds. Waterproof. Not overful, so they wouldn't slop, the muleskinners gently cajoling with their beasts, not pushing them too fast.

They got in line behind the supply wagons, shouting greetings to their friends there until Juan told them to be quiet.

The skies were going a sort of pearly grey with only a blush of sun.

TEN

Dachin said, 'I'm coming down.'

There was little more than darkness now. He knew that the light was failing above the traps. And they were shut as tight as a miser's pouch. From here they were impregnable, could only be opened outside.

They had been feeling their way, him and his two fellow escapees, but so far they had failed: he had to admit this.

They were out of The Pit but just as much incarcerated down here.

He had to feel his way down. He slipped. For a moment he hung, unbalanced, swinging gently then. His arms felt they would pull from his sockets.

One hand slipped from its hold, but then his feet found purchase once more, steadying him. He grabbed with both hands and held on, gasping, the sound magnified in a ghostly way in this black, tomb-like place.

'You makin' it, Clay?'

It was Dulus's voice, and he sounded jittery. He

sounded close also, but it was difficult to tell how close.

'I'll make it.'

'I'll raise my hands.' That was Quane.

The voices sounded hollow, disembodied.

Panting, Dachin got lower. A hand gripped his ankle, pulled. Pulled too hard. 'Goddamit!' Then he was down in a cursing tangle with the other two men.

They sorted themselves out, stood upright, all confessing that they weren't hurt. Dulus was giving out with strange gulps of half laughter, didn't seem to be able to stop. To be able to rise above this, Dachin almost had to shout, after reaching out for Dulus and not finding him.

'There's no way out up there. Everything's tight like a drum and we don't know when it might be opened, do we?'

Dulus was making little sobs. Quane said, 'I guess we gotta go back then, huh?'

'Looks like it.'

'I don't like turning back.'

'Neither do I. But it seems the only thing to do.'

'I want to get out of this place,' said Dulus plaintively.

'We've got to find that gap,' said Dachin.

He could sense the presence of the other two, one to each side of him. 'Stop where you are,' he told them. 'I think I'm facing the gap. I'll walk between you and, when I give the word, you follow.'

'All right,' said Quane, seemingly tractable now.

Dulus didn't say anything. Dachin could hear him breathing deeply.

Dachin moved, said over his shoulder. 'Walk lightly. Don't talk any more. We might be heard as we get nearer to the trapdoor at the other end of the passage.'

'We've got guns,' said Quane. 'If they suspicion we're down here an' get after us we can give a good account of ourselves.'

Dachin walked into the edge of a wall and then around a corner and knew he was in the passage which would lead them out, if they wanted to be out.

Although, in the first place it hadn't seemed to appear so, maybe that way was the best way after all. Certainly better than being trapped in the cavern with the ghostly sound of dripping water. The two men were following him. They both wore soft jail shoes, as he did, scuffed, not too comfortable. Certainly mightily better though than riding boots, for instance, and making only a soft *shush-shush* on the hard floor.

From time to time one or the other of them blundered into the wall of the narrow passage but in the main they proceeded without harm.

It took them longer than any of them could have imagined. Dulus was beginning to breathe hard again as if he was climbing a steep hill. The blackness pressed around them. Dachin began to realize how bad the air was in the passage, and the atmosphere was becoming more tomblike than it had been back in the cavern. But they were committed now.

Suddenly Dachin sensed that there was a wall ahead of him and he stopped dead.

He reached above him and his fingers found the

wooden surface of the inside of the trapdoor.

'Quiet,' he hissed.

The other two had halted as abruptly as he had, and there had been no scuffling.

They listened. 'There's somebody up there,' whispered Quane. And he was right. They all drew their guns.

They could hear the thud of heavy boots above them. Guard's boots. No prisoners wore heavy boots like that. Did any prisoners spend much time in that courtyard? Was it a sort of no-man's land between the main complex and the punishment areas?

Its walls were impregnable: the trio knew that. It's single, small gate was locked and barred on the other side.

They stood, listening, guns in their hands. With his free hand, taking care not to make any noise, Dachin pushed the trap and it gave a little.

Had anybody thought about this tunnel, looked into it even, seeing nothing. Dachin figured that the guards were pretty stupid.

But Captain Hector Ezekiel Stark, the Cap'n – he wasn't stupid. . . .

Still – the footsteps up there were fading. . . .

ELEVEN

Billy Sarmo had some dynamite. He said that the late, elderly powder-man Culey had taught him how to use it, being a friend of his, a helper of Panama Jack as he, Billy, was.

Pity about poor ol' Culey, getting shot like that plumb in the back, and after pulling a fine job also.

Peaboy had to admit that he would have liked Culey along on this second, and more fraught, job of work.

But, as it was, Peaboy would go along with Billy, a reckless personage but, if Culey had taught him right, not likely to go off half-cocked with a load of explosives.

There was a grey twilight as the rumbling procession travelled on, the supply wagons leading the way, the water carts bringing up the rear. The atmosphere was humid, presaging a hot night. The sun had gone but there was not yet any stars or a peeping moon.

In the distance they at last saw the lights of the looming prison known as Stark City. Bitter and cold as a bitch's heart inside, Kelley Rodd had said. And he should know. More than any of them he owed that place a dark vengeance.

He was known there, so kept himself hidden in a wagon. He had chosen his task. With his Winchester he would take care of the lookout guards with their cannons on the towers each side of the huge gates which they hoped would open for them with no trouble at all.

As they were not known in that place Peaboy, Jigger and Bruke did not hide themselves. In fact, their hats pulled down over their eyes they were taking the place of the original guards left behind when the supply train was captured.

Dan and Sep said they weren't known by any of the jail personnel so they patrolled the other side of the train from the gunfighting trio. And they were raring to go.

Billy Sarmo, because of his long association with Caliero where some of the guards caroused from time to time, kept out of sight, taking Kelley Rodd's place with the girls until such time he and his dynamite was needed.

Juan, leader of the muleskinners had picked a perch for himself which suited him fine. He was well known in the prison, even liked; with his fat, jovial personage and his wide grin it was easy for him to ingratiate himself with people, like those 'son-a-bitchin' cattle' as he called the guards.

He perched himself on the seat of the front supply wagon with his shotgun beside him. He said the prison folk had often seen him like that – though he was actually in charge of the water carts he often came to the front like this when they approached the prison – if they'd caught up with each other that is, as they sometimes did: the guards wouldn't see anything unusual in this.

Some of the peons had weapons out of sight. They shuffled along in their usual way. But Juan had said that if things went good for the attackers a lot of the peons would take a hand. They had no reason to be friendly towards the prison folk who treated them like nothing. These peons, would-be *vaqueros*, mule-skinners and storemen would not be easily identi-fied. There were those among them, Injun-like, pure-breeds or half-breeds, *mestizos, caballeros* who had once been fighters and, with the right chances, would fight again.

The wide double gates were opened and the wagon train and its keepers wended their way through while Juan exchanged jocular greetings with guards; and even those in the turrets waved from their perches. The compound which held the water tanks was on the right, conveniently placed, with a wide passage from the gates, the marks of wagon wheels already clear in the soil, the hoofmarks, the footprints.

A few yards from the tanks under their wide well-protected covers were the warehouses where the produce was kept and here the labourers from the wagon train would unload. These doors were already wide open. And the covers were being unbattened, the water tanks revealed, this done by guards. It was then that Peaboy gave the signal, a powerful down-ward sweep of his arm, and guns were drawn and the surprised guards were surrounded.

Other guards had been keeping watch from the guardhouse which, though a little further back than the warehouses, faced the gates and its environs with a clear view.

The watching guards came from their doors as their comrades at the water tanks and the warehouses were being disarmed, their weapons handed to other men who hadn't brought weapons with them, not knowing they needed them – till Peaboy and the others took over out in the badlands.

The guards in the turrets, four all told, became alarmed. But that was when Kelley and Billy got busy with their rifles. Two guards were shot down, others disappeared. Then Billy lit his dynamite sticks and threw them at the guardhouse.

The carnage was violent; and terribly evident. There was shooting on all sides, and hand-to-hand fighting; shocked guards suddenly overcome by an unbelievable nightmare and fearing for their lives at the hands of the furious attackers, fought back desperately. But some of them fled back into the maw of the huge jail to give further alarm.

The trio in the black passage heard heavy feet over their heads again; thudding, but suddenly become faster.

Quane said, 'They're running.'

The thudding, scurrying sounds died. Dachin reached up to the trap, moved it a little. Then all three men heard the explosion.

'Sounds like dynamite,' Dulus said, excitedly.

'Let's get out of here,' said Quane.

'Give me a lift,' Dachin said.

Then, as the echoes of the explosion died, they heard the shooting.

Dachin lifted the trap and poked his head up out of the hole like an inquisitive turtle. He couldn't see anybody. He climbed out of the hole and the other two followed him. He shut the trap, feeling that it wouldn't be wise to leave any signals for anybody who might pass by.

The shooting got louder, as if nearer. Then there was another explosion and this time they saw the smoke over the wall and the ground seemed to vibrate beneath their feet.

'Goda'mighty,' said Quane. 'Somebody left the gate open.'

All their gazes were drawn to that part of the wall and the black smoke drifting above it, thinning. And, beyond that, still gunshots.

The stout narrow door was partially open. Guns in hands, half-crouching warily, they made for this escape hatch.

Out of the hole, which had been getting on his nerves, Dulus talked volubly.

He waved his arm, his fingers semaphoring like an Indian scout's. 'An old convict told me that in the earlier days they had a whippin' post in the middle of this place. But some bigwigs from the East came to look at the prison an' they instructed the Cap'n to take the post away. It's in the cellars now they say and is still used sometimes. There's a lot of underground passages.'

'I guess we picked the wrong one,' Dachin said sardonically.

'Easterners don't worry about what happens here,' Quane said, 'long as it's kept outa sight.'

They were going through the gate. They quit talking. There were sounds of battle ahead. Who needed talk? Action was the watchword now.

TWELVE

Billy Sarmo had thrown more dynamite, with devastating effect. The courtyard was pocked with bodies. With their blockhouse blown apart by the shocking surprise attack from people who were a familiar sight, were often ignored by other guards except the helpers, they were demoralized. They hadn't much cover either.

They scattered in all directions, sought cover, some crouching behind smoking wreckage.

But there was no cover from dynamite unless you could find a hole and burrow yourself in and down deep.

Billy Sarmo, standing erect, had another sputtering stick in his fist when he was hit.

He was spun backwards but hit a cart behind him and was propelled forward again, the dynamite leaving his hand in a looping arc.

Fat Juan was standing at the side of a wagon, long-barrelled handgun in his big fist. His shotgun had proved too slow, with the loading and all, and was leaning against the cart behind him.

The flaming stick landed at Juan's feet and exploded.

The fat man's body, torn horribly, was catapulted in the air and came down in front of what had been the main door of the smouldering blockhouse.

Billy Sarmo, a hole straight through his right shoulder, lay on his back, half-on and half-off the cart, lost consciousness. At the same time, below him the young gunny called Dan was hit in the throat, his triumphant yells choked there, his life taken from him.

A sort of wail went up from the native attackers at the loss of their genial leader, and everybody's *amigo*, Juan. He had been like a bosom uncle to many of them and had left back in Caliero a plump and pretty wife and two growing kids, a boy and a girl.

The wails and imprecations rose to a roar and the attackers, throwing caution to the winds, surged forward. The guards backed, sought more cover.

They had scored. They had seen the death of a leader (though some of them had liked him, and they had seen the ferocious dynamiter brought down. But, callous and selfish men, they weren't paid to throw their lives away. They weren't soldiers, and most of them had never pretended to be. They were bully-boys, gunmen, sadists, some of them actually fugitives from the law they had recently served, hiding, working out their frustrations on helpless prisoners at the behest of a loco figure called Cap'n.

He appeared. With a carbine in one hand, a pistol in the other. He stood yelling his troops on; crimson-faced he was, and pop-eyed, not now an inspiring sight.

75

He fired off his guns, but whether he hit anything was a moot point. Then, as if he had been merely an apparition, he disappeared.

Peaboy, Jigger and Bruke had kept each other in sight and, so far, none of them had been hit. Kelley Rodd was in the small wagon where the two girls were crouching and he busy with his rifle, more of a crackshooter than anybody had at first expected him to be, a dark horse now kicking back at the folk who had done him wrong. The young gunfighter called Sep had run to check his friend Dan and found him beyond help. He was now down on one knee beside the body and had a Colt in each hand, was aiming and triggering methodically as if at a turkey shoot or a braggin' contest with bullets.

Some of the guards had found cover, were retaliating. Others were backing. And they backed into trouble. Three men in grey prison garb but armed with guns and using them methodically.

One guard, turning, received a slug full in the face: his jaw had dropped, and then he lost it: his death was quick and bloody.

A companion, whirling, gun lifting, was hit in the belly and collapsed, writhing and screaming, a sound to curdle a man's insides.

In a lull a voice was shouting, 'Clay! Over here, Clay.'

Clay Dachin, with his two fellow-escapees, Quane and Dulus, pressed forward.

Quane was suddenly hit in the side of the head with what might have been a stray bullet. He cried out and spun, dropping his gun, his eyes rolling till he hit the ground, and then becoming blank. The other two saw that they could do nothing for him, hastened to join their deliverers.

An unarmed guard who had obviously lost his gun and was half-crazy, his face streaming with blood, flung himself at Dachin. The latter used his gun like a whip, knocking the man unconscious to the ground.

But most of the guards had no more fight left in them, were looking for places to hide. And they certainly knew this honeycombed penal settlement better than the visitors did.

The peons and muleskinners, still mad at the death of Juan and other comrades, were sacking the place. They were taking all valuables and money they could find. This was their time to howl – and enrich themselves in the process. Who could blame them?

Somebody had got hold of some keys and prisoners were being let loose. Somebody else said fires had started. There was smoke in various places.

An exodus was beginning. Dead and wounded were gathered up. In the small wagon, a little Mexican *puta* wept. A special male friend of hers had been killed.

She was comforted by her partner, and by marksman Kelley Rodd who didn't bear even a scratch.

Clay Dachin, while thanking Peaboy and Jigger for their great help – and the mighty backing of their allies – was surprised to see big Bruke.

He had expected the other two to turn up sooner or later but he hadn't expected Bruke. The big man had received a bullet-crease in the side of his head

77

and was kind of punch-drunk, hugged Dachin like a drunken man, his eyes owlish.

The procession was on its way, going back the way it had come. Prisoners, begging food, full canteens, were scattering, taking their chances in the badlands. Some had friends among the populace of Caliero, were taking a chance of hiding there for a while.

Billy Sarmo, his plump face glistening with sweat, his smashed shoulder roughly but heavily bandaged, said, 'I don't know what Panama Jack's gonna say about that.'

Dachin had been in a conflab with Peaboy and Jigger. He had another helper too, who didn't seem to want to leave his side. Dulus, his fellow-prisoner from The Pit.

Clay, legendary gunfighter and leader of men was in command again. He said, 'Panama Jack owes us now. He'll do as he's told.'

Part Two

THE SEARCH

THIRTEEN

He was born over the borders of Texas, in Louisiana. He didn't have a Texas accent, not what you'd call a deeply Western one. Neither did he have a Southern accent, though he could put on the coat of a 'Southern geenulman', if he chose. He was a man of many parts. In a nutshell, he was a ruthless killer who was loyal to his friends.

He was a charmer – even confidence man Kelley Rodd couldn't wholly beat him at that. He was more handsome than Kelley, and a mite younger too.

Women loved him. Men followed him but were wary of him.

Though still a young man he had seen more of the bitterness and seamy side of life than many men twice his age – and many women, unless they were wildcats.

His father had died in a saloon brawl and he, the only son, had been too young to avenge that death in the feudal way. This had been done by an uncle, who came and went, unattached, he and his boys on the owlhoot trail.

His mother had been a woman who had to have a man. She had been faithful to the boy's father, had

grieved for him. But there are many ways of assuag-
ing guilt and, eventually, she took an easy one,
comforting herself with other men.

The boy had a succession of 'uncles' who helped
on the good farm which had been the father's pride
and joy, until he had been bitten by the gambling
bug which, ultimately, brought about his death.

Some of the 'uncles' weren't bad. They worked the
boy but were good to him: he didn't resent all of
them, only a few. They sent him to the local school.
Then came the man called Teal who had been a
teacher. He taught the boy many things before he,
finally, like the others, went on his way.

The one who took his place was the worst of all,
and he was the one the mother, a pretty woman still
but no longer a filly, decided to marry. An older man
than the others, a smirking, burly, smooth-talker, a
ram who turned into a wolf also.

He did little work. As the boy got older and
stronger he was the one who was left to do the work.
The woman became sick with her insides, maybe her
heart. The man did not treat her well. The boy
watched.

He did not feel for his mother like he used to do.
He had gotten himself educated. In so many ways.

The man began to strike out at him, blows he
usually evaded, thrown as they were in drink as the
man boozed more and more. Despite the boy's
efforts, the farm began to fall into a dilapidated state.

The boy's notorious uncle called from time to
time, watchful, scornful, he and his boys usually on
the run.

And the man came home drunk one too many times and cornered the boy in a broken-down barn and came at him with a buggy-whip: he had sold the buggy long since.

The boy was suddenly no longer a boy. He fought back.

He had learned to use his fists. In an area where some folks and their offspring had been heard to call the boy's mother a whore, your new father a booze-hound, you had to maintain your feudal rights the hard way.

The youth told himself afterwards that he hadn't meant to kill the man. . . . He had grasped the buggy-whip and, with his other hand, had struck the man on the angle of his jaw. The man had fallen, had hit his head on a broken ploughshare, part of the dusty rubbish that littered the place, the signs of neglect.

In his later years, the boy had thought of this as a sort of poetic justice. But, when the thing happened, he had no notion of that. A man's head had been split apart: a man had died.

His mother had told him to run and he had refused. Still fiercely loyal, he hadn't wanted her to be blamed for anything. He said he would take the body on his horse into town and tell the sheriff the story.

The sheriff was sick, the woman said. But the youth, strong and determined, did what he had planned. But then the malicious fates, masters of coincidence, took a hand in things.

Even as the youth climbed into the saddle, the body swathed in a blanket in front of him, two of the dead man's erstwhile cronies rode up, and there were others coming across the prairie: some sort of a shindig had been planned and they were there to take the man with them.

They took the boy. They had already been drinking from ready bottles as they rode. They locked the screaming woman in the house They took her son out to a nearby conveniently shaped tree and they strung him up.

The Fates had done their worst. But maybe he had a guardian angel too, a masculine one. He came in the shape of favourite uncle. And with his boys, he came well-armed with firepower.

In the mêlée a half-drunken townie was shot dead. The youth, now running with the outlaw gang, was blamed for that second killing as well as that of the stepfather. A price was put on his head – there were already reward dodgers out on the outlaw uncle and his followers. Thus began the legend of Clay Dachin, gunfighting killer.

They did a few jobs while he only held the horses: a bank in Fort Worth; an express office in Waco; a stage station carrying gold from San Antonio. They travelled widely, working their way down to the borderlands.

The leader, Chuck Mentone, who was young Clay's mother's brother, had a price on his head as did most of his followers, five all told now, counting Chuck's nephew, the horse-holder. Sometimes Chuck hired extra men, picking them carefully. But he preferred to use his regulars: seasoned owlhooters of his own generation. Clay was by far the youngest among them now.

Chuck Mentone, a seasoned professional at what he did, famous for his keen planning, abhorred too much violence or killing.

In the bank at Waco, the bank guard and clerks disarmed, a reckless client with a big gun took a chance, pinked one of the boys in the shoulder. Then he was brought down by a bullet from another bandit.

It was later learned that the man had died in hospital, and Chuck didn't like that, particularly as his orders had been no shooting.

The raid went off without a hitch. They'd had inside information and the express office jockey was as co-operative as a cathouse madam with fillies to spare.

The San Antonio stage job, which actually took place on a trail between that near-border town and Waco, was not so easy. Chuck had learned that the wagon guards were planning a rip-off themselves – and he figured to get in first. There was a gun-battle in which two guards were killed and one of Chuck's men also.

The robbers got away with the loot, but now they were one man short. Chuck agreed that his nephew, Clay, who had been pestering the hide off him for a more important role than holding horses' heads, should take the dead man's place. But something else had been bothering Clay, and Chuck let him get on with this first, while taking great care in doing so: visiting his mother.

Arriving by twilight after making a wide circuit of the town where he was known, he found the farm as dilapidated as when he had left, if not even more so.

He found his mother in a drunken stupor with her latest man, who was even more drunk than she was, could only curse and mumble at the visitor while the woman looked on with bleary eyes.

This raddled wreck of a woman clad only in a dirty, threadbare shift was not the mother Clay remembered. He left the two of then as they were and rode back the way he had come and without incident.

He caught up with the boys in Ellsworth. And that was where the whole bunch, making their way out, were ambushed by a law party. These badged deputies were led by a Marshal Gillie, notorious for being reluctant to take prisoners. A deputy was killed; so were two of Chuck Mentone's bunch, though he and his nephew escaped unscathed, as did the rest except for one with a busted arm (he'd fallen off his horse), which subsequently healed.

The man took a mighty load of joshing about his ineptitude. But deep down the boys were sad, their morale kind of low.

Eventually, Chuck picked up a couple of partners he had used before. Names: Jigger and Peaboy: a small brown man fast with a gun; and a tall, lean, powerful-looking one who did tricks with a knife but was pretty good also with everything warlike and lethal.

Chuck needed replacements: he already had another job planned before they all took a rest – Jigger and Peaboy included – and, as their leader sardonically put it, 'made use of their ill-gotten gains in any way they chose for themselves'.

During his horse-holding days when he had plenty of time on his hands Clay Dachin had started to keep a journal in an old tally book he had found.

He had been raring to go, get into things more with the boys, but, at the same time, he had been wondering how long he would stay in this game (and a sort of a game it had been for him then) even if Uncle Chuck began to give him a greater share in things. And Chuck ultimately did this of course. But at odd times Clay still kept on with his journal. Way back, a teacher had told him that he 'wrote well'.

None of the boys – and some of them could barely write their own names – dared to josh him about what they referred to as his 'diary' not long after, a brawny lad fast as a cougar, he had floored one of the boys who had prowess with his own maulies. Clay had put him down like a poleaxed bull. They became comrades afterwards, though: Chuck Mentone saw to that.

Chuck never stole from folk who couldn't afford to be robbed, folk whom he thought of as his own kind. He, like many other owlhooters had taken to that trail after the Civil War with no home to go back to, no parents (the father killed fighting, the mother dying with consumption brought about by malnutrition), only a sister who got married and went off with her man.

Chuck, almost like an Indian, purely hated trains. To him they were the noisy, smoking symbols of hated Easterners, 'Yankees', and slimy, fat-bellied carpet-baggers, He had never done a train. He purely needed to do a train before he and the boys took it easy for a while.

Perhaps his genial eagerness made him careless, not a usual trait of his. Word must have got out somehow about an impending attack on an 'iron horse' that was carrying bullion, and the rich mine-owner who owned it, towards the East. It had guards, of course, but Chuck figured his boys could handle those bastards and their Eastern masters.

Things didn't go at all as planned, however. Marshal Gillie and his posse were waiting, having got their information from an ex-member of Chuck Mentone's gang and subsequently a Gillie deputy, who had picked it up through careless talk in a bordello by one of Chuck's boys. It was never clear who this was. But the cathouse girl had passed on the information to another client, who happened to be the ex-outlaw who'd become a deputy, his name being Lickramer, a moniker not easily forgotten.

During the terrible, abortive raid, Clay Dachin saw some of his comrades killed. And, most harrowing of all, he saw his Uncle Chuck shot in the back, done to death by a flaming Colt in the hand of Marshal Gillie.

Dachin escaped, and with him were Jigger and Peaboy.

Later, Dachin went off alone on a trail of vengeance. He caught ex-outlaw informant Lickramer in Fort Worth and killed him in a stand-up gunfight, not receiving even a scratch himself.

He braced Marshal Gillie, a married man but with no offspring, as he was leaving the home of his mistress, a sprightly widow in a small town. None of the marshal's deputies were near, or likely to be.

Two fast gunfighters faced each other on a dusty street as the sun was going down. This was a quiet, law-abiding town called Jeromeville which became famous through what happened there that quiet evening when the shattering cacophony of gunfire destroyed the peace.

Marshal Gillie lay flat on his back with a bullet hole between his eyes. And the dark, lean, blue-eyed young man who had killed him in a fair fight got back on to his own horse and rode away.

He had a flesh wound in his upper arm. He went to join his two partners Jigger and Peaboy. He rested up while his wound healed, and in that time the story of the two gunfights spread and the legend of Clay Dachin grew apace.

FOURTEEN

They did a couple of quick jobs because they needed the money.

They worked the way Chuck Mentone had done. Clay, the acknowledged leader, wouldn't have had it any other way. All three of them were still young, but Clay was the most mature. He was also the fastest with a gun, faster even than small, brown, fidgety-mean Jigger.

Peaboy, tall, lean, muscular was, like Clay, a quiet one. With a handgun he wasn't as fast as the other one, but he was crack with a rifle, the fastest ever until, years on, he met confidence-man ex-con Kelley Rodd. Anyway, Peaboy was more adept with a knife than anybody the others had ever seen.

Peaboy backed Dachin, as time went on almost seemed to read his thoughts.

On the first two jobs, they worked as a three-man team, not wanting to use anybody else. Nobody got hurt. A small bank. A class emporium. In and out like greased cats, leaving folks still with their hands over their heads and stupefied looks on their faces, not having seen the faces of the trio who had robbed them, only bandannas and fiery eyes, while harsh voices barked at them menacingly. Jigger was the best at the menacing voice ploy, and he had eyes like a polecat.

In the time-honoured way, after the second job the boys went their separate ways, agreeing to meet in a certain place at a certain time on a particular day.

Clay had a girl, daughter of a widowed man, ex-outlaw, who had been an old friend of Chuck Mentone.

This elderly man was straight now, for the most part making a frugal living buying and selling horses from a medium sized one-storey cabin in a valley sheltered by cottonwoods. It was a lonely place and thus a calling point for folks on the run, or resting up after a spot of larceny. The horse dealer took them in, asked no questions. That was friendship, succour, means for getting some extra *dinero*, if a caller had such to spare, free handout if he hadn't.

The man was fiercely protective of his pretty, dark-haired daughter. But she loved Clay Dachin and her father couldn't do anything about it, ultimately didn't want to, found himself liking the quiet young man with the courteous flavour of the South about his manners, even his speech sometimes, a cajoling note.

When Clay ealled, the father Jabez Snow made himself scarce, went to buy or sell some horses, leaving his daughter Della and her love alone, knowing the girl would come to no harm. Soon Jabez knew the tales about Clay Dachin, killer gunfighter. But he

91

took the man at face value, said it didn't do to believe everything you heard. Jabe affirmed, with his throaty chuckle, that he didn't claim to be any damn' angel himself.

Della knew that Clay had other girls. He was a young man who drew womenfolk to him. But she knew in her bones that he would always return to her: he had told her so and she believed him.

Jigger went over the border where he had a Mexican sweetheart. Peaboy took women as he found them, sometimes didn't even bother, preferring a smoky barroom and a deck of cards in his silky fingers.

As they lay together, Della told Clay that she was expecting a child. It was something they hadn't expected, hadn't wanted. But now the girl was blooming and, though she wasn't showing any signs yet of the pregnancy, he thought he had never seen her look so beautiful. He sensed without being told that she would welcome the child after all.

But in the dark eyes that looked up at him there was the shadow of a lingering doubt and he knew that the doubt was about him. He was a roving star. What would he want with a child?

Usually his thoughts were shrewd, quick. But now he spoke hardly without hearing the words coming from his mouth as if they had blossomed deeply inside him and had been forced out.

'We'll get married. I'll get some more money and then we will get married.'

'I'd like that, Clay,' she said softly.

He felt himself smiling, said, 'It was in the cards I

guess. This place could be turned into something much better y'know. More horses, some cattle and other livestock, more buildings.'

'I'd like that too,' she said. 'And so would Dad, I'm sure of it.'

'I'll have to talk to him. That's the thing to do, ain't it?'

But old Jabez was willing all right, knowing though that Clay would have to be on his way again and whatever happened later would still be in the lap of the gods. His own wife, Della's mother, had died giving birth to the girl. Della had never known her mother and Jabez hadn't taken up with another woman since. Not permanently anyway, only sometimes when he was off on one of his buying and selling trips.

When Della was born he was off on a trip but it hadn't been for buying or selling, it had been for stealing. It was something he would never forget, for he had loved that woman. He tried to push that from his mind and look to the future.

Maybe he had once dreamed of a different spouse for his lovely daughter. She had known other men, but she had never looked at any man the way she looked at Clay. The way her mother used to look at Jabez when their love was young. He had planned to give up the owlhoot, but he had left it too late.

Watching the young horseman ride away, Della waving, he hoped and prayed Clay would not make the same mistake. But neither of them could foresee the future.

When Dachin got to the rendezvous, Jigger was already there. He said he had left the border town where his *chiquita* lived earlier, and quicker than he usually did.

While Jigger was away, his *chiquita* had had another man. The sardonic little fellow didn't blame her too much for that, but he objected most strongly to the other jasper, a full-blood Mex, a handsome *caballero* horning in while the girl was with her faithful inamorato. She and Jigger had known each other since they were kids and had shared their first sexual experiences together.

The *caballero* hadn't realized that the girl's small long-time lover was a veritable wildcat when aroused. Jigger demonstrated this aspect of his nature and the fact that he was much stronger than he looked by throwing the young man through a bedroom window, breaking various parts of his anatomy in the process.

The young man had two brothers, noted *pistoleros* who came after Jigger with blood in their eyes. He beat a hasty retreat. 'Should've had you with me, *amigo*,' he said now.

'Do you think those two are still after you?'

'Nah, I don't think so. I think I shook 'em off purty well.'

Dachin didn't say anything else on the subject. He had been in a similar predicament himself, a far more horrendous one than that experienced by his small friend.

A young woman who kept a small store in a town where he had sojourned had told him she was a widow. She had two kids, real bright buttons. She and Clay had become very close. He had liked the kids too.

Her husband, who had been doing a stretch in Yuma – the kids and the townsfolk didn't know that – suddenly turned up as if out of nowhere.

The woman hadn't wanted her man back. He had brutalized her before he had been jailed for beating a man almost to death for being little more than pleasant to the wife.

He had been insanely jealous. After his incarceration the woman had tried to shut him out of her life, her thoughts, and that was why she had told the children that he would never return. They hardly remembered him anyway. She had called herself a widow, running the small store she had managed to rent and make prosper, shutting herself and the children away in this small town where she didn't think she would be found.

But he found her. And he was still her husband. And it came as quite a shock to the woman's short-time paramour, Clay Dachin, to learn that she wasn't a widow after all.

In an upstairs room, the husband had drawn a gun on the man who was with his wife, had threatened to shoot them both. Clay Dachin was no idiot. He believed what the man said and, not knowing the full reason for the deception, was disgusted that he'd been in what was now a pretty hurtful tight corner.

It could be a fatal one.

The woman was calling to the man by name, pleading with him. The man lashed out at her with the gun. She backed. He missed. His eyes blazing maniacally. he went after her, momentarily taking his gaze away from her companion.

Dachin moved. The husband whirled towards him but wasn't fast enough. The sweeping fist caught him on the angle of the jaw, a beautifully placed blow with a lot of muscle behind it.

He went down, his eyes turning up then closing, his gun slipping from his grasp.

Clay Dachin got out of there.

As the man regained consciousness, his wife shot him. Then she set the place on fire, store, everything, and she escaped with the kids. Clay Dachin did not hear of any of this till afterwards and there was still mystery attached to the event. Woman and children seemed to have vanished. And there was only the charred body of the man with a bullet hole in his head to bear witness to what had happened in that upstairs room. A poor witness.

There were people who had known of the woman's association with that gunfighting killer Clay Dachin, and they thought he'd make a much better witness than a blackened corpse, mute as a tombstone. It was as if Dachin had spirited the woman and the two children into oblivion. It was another crime to place at his door.

FIFTEEN

Dachin did not remind Jigger of the incident with the store woman and her spouse, though the small man knew of the circumstances and had not commented on them either one way or the other at any time. Dachin had the feeling that Jigger might now be regreting that he had run away from the vengeful brothers and, not only that, regretted that he had told Dachin about it.

Or maybe Jigger had just made an error of judgement about the running and the losing of the two followers.

And this latter proved to be the case.

Peaboy still hadn't turned up, and his two waiting partners were walking down the main street of the rendezvous town when the two burly Mexicans appeared ahead of them and stopped, facing them.

'I never thought. . . .' Then Jigger was speechless. But Dachin knew a stand-up challenge when he saw it and had acted accordingly.

Jigger and the two brothers were all given a demonstration of the lightning draw that was already legendary in the West. The two brothers, hands only at the butts of their guns stood as if frozen, a still picture under the blaze of the sun.

Jigger had his gun half out of its holster. At his side, Dachin had the steel finger of his own Colt levelled at the two men. Jigger drew his gun all the way.

Dachin said, 'Unbuckle your gunbelts carefully, my friends, and let them fall.'

The men's dark eyes were flickering as if they were planning a daring grandstand play. But the one who looked the older said something out of the corner of his mouth to his brother while unbuckling his own belt at the same time. The younger man followed suit and his gun thudded to the sunbaked ground.

Dachin said quietly to Jigger, 'Get behind 'em an' pick that stuff up. See if they've got anything else.'

Jigger moved lightly, even snakelike in his dark smallness. He circled the brother who stood a little apart and they raised their hands when Dachin told them to do so. Jigger kept his gun in his right hand, straight and ready, thumb on the hammer. He used his left hand deftly and came up with a couple of knives and two back-up guns – a double-bore derringer and an ornate little pistol which looked a bit like a kid's toy but obviously wasn't. These two were a mite fancy-looking but they wouldn't carry baubles.

Jigger slung the gunbelt over his shoulder, complete with the heavy Colts. He stashed the other gear about his person and sashayed sideways back to Dachin, manoeuvring instinctively out of the line of fire and still keeping the brothers covered. They

98

could have been put down but Jigger sensed that Clay didn't want it that way. With Peaboy still missing they couldn't afford to draw too much attention to themselves in this town.

Already folks were gathering, staring, but, wisely, not coming too near.

Dachin got a little closer to the two men and the older one asked, 'Can we put our hands down?' The other one hadn't said a word.

'All right,' said Dachin, almost gently. 'But keep 'em away from your sides.'

Again the older one growled something sidelong to his brother. They both lowered their hands slowly, staring with dark hate at the two Anglos with levelled shooters in front of them.

Dachin said, 'I want you to turn around and lead us back to where you stashed your horses.'

The younger man spoke for the first time, shortly, pungently, in Spanish. The words sounded like spitting and were so rapid that even Jigger, who wasn't as Anglo as his companion and could speak at least bastardized Spanish, the sort used in the borderlands, couldn't understand what was said. It wasn't complimentary, though.

'Move,' said Dachin.

They moved, turning around, walked with a swagger as if still full of arrogance. Jigger felt like blasting them down. But he, even he, had never shot a man in the back. And he knew his friend Clay wasn't about to do that. If those two had been on the hoof after a raid, getting away, well, that would be a different matter. . . .

Jigger, an illiterate man, had heard of the code of the West, was puzzled by it, wondered if it had ever really existed. The brothers went on with their swaggering march and Jigger and his erudite friend brought up the rear.

A few townies tagged along but kept well back. The word had got around. A gunfight? Nah, there'd been no shooting! Some folks were relieved about that. This wasn't exactly a shooting-type town. Some of the barflies were peeved at not seeing something more violent. At least it would be something to talk about.

Some had gone back to their cups, their cards, their chores. Heads still peeped from windows and doors here and there. There was no sign of law. The local marshal, a veteran who was running to fat, didn't move very fast, would have reacted to a spate of shooting, but not much else.

The brothers marched past the livery station and on to the end of town. Somebody ventured to remark that maybe the two men with guns were federal marshals or something and the two prisoners were Mexican *bandidos*.

'Nah,' said the inevitable barfly who knew everything. 'Those two gunfighters are Clay Dachin and his partner called Jigger. There's usually a third one called Peaboy or somep'n funny like that. You don't mess with any o' them boys anyway, old hoss.'

The brothers' horses were looped to trees just outside of town ready for a quick getaway. Dachin instructed them to 'Go back where you came from. If we see you again we will kill you.' He slapped the horses' flanks, sent them galloping on their way.

The two partners, the smaller one still festooned with commandeered armoury, watched them till the dust settled and then there was nothingness.

'Do you think they'll come back?' asked Jigger.

'Maybe. But we did the best we had to do.'

'Yeh.'

As they got back in town Peaboy rode in from the other direction. He was perky as usual, apologized for being late, said he had some news he figured might interest them.

SIXTEEN

They were way out of town when Jigger voiced something that seemed to be worrying him, though he wasn't usually the worrying kind.

'Clay, them two brothers didn't have rifles on them hosses o' their'n. There was no sheaths on their saddles for them either.'

'Maybe they just didn't have rifles.'

'Everybody has rifles. I was wondering whether they had stashed 'em someplace else, scabbards an' all.'

They had told Peaboy about the brothers. He said, 'You can take them saddle-scabbards off and tote 'em with the long gun. Mine comes off; look.'

His rifle-scabbard was attached to his saddle with buckles.

'I was thinkin',' said Jigger. 'Maybe those boys've got rifles. An' I was thinking there's them bluffs up ahead on this trail. Dandy place for a drygulch parlay.'

'We don't have to stay on this main trail,' said Peaboy. 'We can veer off. I know of a quicker way to get to where we're aimin' for.'

'Them two boys didn't actually ride off this way,' said Dachin, but he sounded doubtful, figuring now they could have made a detour, come in on the other side of town. If they had had rifles and Jigger was right (he probably was!) they could have left them at a rooming-house or with a friend, a friendly whore maybe, ready to pick up later.

They'd been run out of town by Jigger and Dachin and the latter thought now, yeh, I should've wondered about rifles, what in hell was wrong with my head?

'All right,' he said to Peaboy. 'Take the route you fancy.'

Peaboy led the way. They caught up with him and the three of them rode abreast, a comfortable space between them.

Nobody shot at them. They didn't see a living soul. The sun was going down and the temperature had dropped.

They rode easy. They went over again what Peaboy had told them.

They got to the town they sought in the late night the way Peaboy had had it figured.

Dachin was going along with that. Jigger wasn't worrying about anything now, just wanted to get the job done.

Dachin suddenly said, 'I've got a cousin lives here.'

It was as if he'd just thought of it. But Jigger and Peaboy didn't know whether their taciturn and some-times enigmatic pard hadn't realized the fact all along, hadn't bothered to mention it.

'Oh,' said Peaboy mockingly, 'you want to go visitin' then?'

Dachin seemed to give the question some thought then said, 'Too dark. Besides, we want to get in an' out sharp, don't we?'

Jigger wasn't sure who was mocking who. 'Who's that then, Clay?' he asked.

'Feller named Jeremiah Bruke. Keeps a store with his widowed mother. Everybody calls him just Bruke. Even I always have. We used to be close when we were tads.'

'I think I've been in that,' said Peaboy. 'Once. Big genial feller. Dry goods store.'

'That's the place. That's Bruke. Wouldn't hurt a mouse.'

'That ain't the place we want anyway,' said Peaboy caustically. 'It's a leetle ahead. Dark now. Almost next to that lighted buildin' with the false front and the lights downstairs. That's a rathskellar. There're still a few folks comin' out. . . . The jail's at the other of the street,' he added as if an afterthought.

'Pull into the shadows,' Clay Dachin said.

They didn't move till things were quiet and the lights in the tall pleasure house went out. And then this seemed like a mighty peaceful town.

They went up a convenient alley beside the squat, tightly built building that Peaboy had first indicated. They left the town at the other end of the alley where they would look out on privies and rubbish. But no privies right opposite luckily, not so much danger of anybody with a quick call dashing out, ass on fire, as

104

Peaboy put it.

Peaboy hissed, 'They've got a gun-guard like I said. But this is his night for whoring. He'll be down at the cathouse till the early hours. I did my pokin' and listenin' prime.'

'I guess you did,' said Jigger in a throaty whisper.

Dachin didn't say anything. You had to prove things to him. Besides, he didn't like talking on a job. So now Peaboy did some demonstrating.

The boys hadn't taken into account what an Eastern newsman might have referred to as 'unforeseen circumstances'.

Although they didn't know it then, they were to come upon more than their foreseeable share of such circumstance in the far from distant future. . . .

But they were on with their task, Jigger a bit behind the other two and keeping watch, Dachin close by Peaboy at the stout back door. Peaboy used a slim iron bar, flattened at the end, the edges razor sharp. It was one of his favourite tools of nefarious intent, of which he had a prime collection.

The door gave in. With a loud crack. And the three men froze. A cat crossed before them in the wishy-washy moonlight, nose in air, disdaining them; disappeared.

Peaboy pushed the door open without even a creak. The trio, as one, blew out their breath in relief. Then they were inside, and Jigger closed the door carefully behind them.

'Like I said,' hissed Peaboy, 'I have the combination of the safe. I have eyes like a hawk, you boys know that. I memorized the numbers from the counter while I watched the clerk put my important papers away, after I'd learned that the bank always puts clients' important things in the money-safe. A special concession they call it. Hell, they ain't had no crookery here in a coon's age.'

'You talk too much,' said Dachin.

'I talked myself into that all right,' retorted Peaboy. 'They think I'm gonna be a big client, a new cattleman with a big bundle to stash with 'em when it's all collected up.'

'A big un' 'ull change hands all right,' chuckled Jigger.

'Anyway,' said Peaboy, aiming at Dachin. 'This is the gun-guard's place out back an' he ain't gonna be here. There's nobody can hear us talking. . . . This way.'

Pale moonlight came through the window, illuminating their way if they trod carefully. It was part of their nature that they all had a gun out. But held by their sides. They were professionals who weren't about to use a shooter unless they definitely needed to do that. Noisy things, guns, Peaboy had said, who much preferred a knife.

The windows in front of the bank were covered by dark curtains, something else Peaboy had noted. The safe was way behind the counter so they were able to light a fairly low-hanging desk lantern and use this for illumination.

Anyway, it didn't take Peaboy long to open the safe and he brought small canvas sacks out of his vest, four all told, one each and one left over. And they needed all of them, filling three of them with bills and gold coins and then going round the office and picking up enough odd *dinero* to make the fourth one bulge.

They were ready to leave and they were riding high. But they were about to experience a comedown that they couldn't, even in the realms of conjecture, anticipate.

They didn't know that the bank guard, an ex-lawman whom everybody called Abe, had an attack of the croup but, even so had made his way down to the cathouse on this, his usual night. Before much time had elapsed, however, he had become decidedly unwell and two of the girls had insisted on helping him back home.

In case any nosy townsfolk happened to still be around in main street or maybe out on their stoops in the cool of the night, the girls had decided to lead Abe along the backs of town. And thus that trio, two girls and a half-inebriated, sick man reached the back door of the bank just as another trio, all male and toting and armed to the teeth, were quitting it.

The girls let Abe go and he banged against the wall beside the door, slumped into a sitting position, head sunk on chest, and passed out completely.

'Take care of him, girls,' Dachin said. 'We have to be on our way.'

But, unfortunately, Jigger, still sticking to his earler position as look-out, had his gun in his hand and the girl saw it. One of them opened her mouth as if to scream and Dachin clapped his hand over it.

'We're not gonna hurt you, honey,' he said, in a deep gentle voice. 'We just want to be on our way quietly, y'know.'

He let her go. Her eyes were bright and scared in the pale moonlight, but her lips were pressed tightly together.

The three boys passed on. And then something completely unexpected happened. The second girl, who had been as quiet as a scared mouse, suddenly drew a small, double-barrelled derringer and let fly.

In the dark stillness the report of the gun sounded like that of a small cannon. Peaboy almost dropped his boodle, managed to retain it while keeping a hand free which he clapped to his ear, crying in astonishment, 'Goddamn, I'm hit!' But then all three of them were running.

Still, the reckless cathouse frail let off the second barrel of her little gun.

With their well-developed instinct for self-preservation, the men were half-crouching as they moved and, in any case, the second slug went way over their heads. Then they were around the corner in the alley and mounting their horses. Both girls began to scream, awakening the echoes, and the hammer of hasty hoofs created a cacophony to wake a town and, as the three men looked back, lights were blossoming.

SEVENTEEN

Peaboy hadn't had time to do anything for his wounded ear and, as they rode at a breakneck pace, the fury of their passage caused the blood to whip behind him like a wind blown red scarf. He was cursing monotonously.

'Stow it,' Jigger yelled. 'I guess that ain't no more'n a goddamn flea-bite.'

Things had gone haywire. But at least they had the boodle.

Peaboy had told them about the law in that town. He had been thorough. It wasn't exactly a tough, lawless place: just kind of wild at times as most Western townships were.

It had what might be called a good sheriff, and two deputies. They were all middle-aged, but seasoned. They didn't bother about minor peccadilloes. They didn't have much to do, so probably had gotten fairly indolent.

But Peaboy had figured that it wouldn't do to sell them short. They were conscientious and bigger trouble would rouse them. They might even sort of welcome it.

So now they had to figure that pretty soon they would have a posse on their heels: disappointing after the quiet care they'd taken. They hadn't harmed a soul and, for sure, a crazy cathouse frail with a derringer was the last thing they had expected.

Peaboy had ignored Jigger's gibe. But now he shouted, 'I've got to fix this ear or I'm gonna bleed to death or somep'n. There're some low hills just ahead.'

'All right,' said Dachin. 'We'll bide a mite. But don't take too long.'

'I won't.'

'I'll stand look-out,' grumbled Jigger.

They reached the hills and halted in a dip surrounded by craggy boulders, a good ambush point should they need one. But they didn't aim to run head-on into trouble if they could avoid it. After all, they were not a bunch of gun-crazy youngsters.

Dachin took a look at Peaboy's ear, said the slug had taken the lobe off; there was a ragged mess. But the wound wasn't bleeding so badly.

'My shirt at that side is soaked,' whined Peaboy. 'I ought to change.'

'We ain't got time for you to change your damn' shirt,' snapped Dachin.

'I've got one in my—' Peaboy was interrupted by derisive laughter from Jigger who, though standing look-out, was within earshot.

Dachin bandaged Peaboy's ear, making him look like some kind of gargoyle in the night. Then, under

110

the pale moon, the trio rode on. Jigger said he hadn't heard anything. But the night was still, with no wind to carry sound. They came out of the edge of the hills, skirted them, hoping that would fool pursuers who would slow down in case of ambush.

Dachin had the proceeds of the robbery on his saddle. Jigger was still somewhat overloaded with weaponry he had taken from the two Mexican brothers, said he'd sell some of it someplace but hadn't got around to that yet.

Peaboy, being wounded, was relatively unencumbered otherwise; a good thing as they didn't want their ill-gotten gains to get all bloody.

The hard riding had caused his wound to start bleeding again, the bandage a sodden red rag, his shirt little better. 'I ought to see a sawbones,' he said. And this time his two pards agreed with him.

After a little more riding, Peaboy cursing, sounding weaker, Dachin said, 'There's a little settlement over to the right there.' He jerked a thumb.

Jigger said, 'I know it.'

'You two go there, get that ear fixed up. I'll go on, hide this stuff. I guess it would be best we split up anyway. Those two whores saw three of us.'

They agreed on a place to meet. They split up.

It was some time before Dachin realized that, though they were still pretty far back, a bunch of horsemen were following his trail.

He had a good horse, but the beast had been ridden hard and his pace was flagging somewhat.

He veered off the trail he had been following.

Over to the right of him were more hills. He avoided them. He knew of another town where he might hide among the shanties, a bigger place than where he had sent his two partners so that Peaboy could get his ear quickly seen to. But not much bigger, and a miserable place since a small silver mine nearby had petered out.

He reached the place, ghostly silent under the pale moon. He found an empty shack with a sagging broken roof and he paused there, got down and put his ear to the ground. There was a vibration, maybe hoofbeats, he couldn't be sure. Were there riders and, if so, how many?

Were they smarter than he had expected them to be?

He entered the shack. The moon gave him a bit of light and, after all the setbacks, Lady Luck smiled on him at last. He found a shovel, rusty, only half a handle. But useable.

He buried the sacks with the boodle and strewed rubbish over the place. It would be even better if the shack fell upon this dirt floor as it looked as if it might do.

As he came out of the sagging open door of the shack two men were waiting for him and he recognized then immediately. The two Mexican brothers he had sent running so recently, and yet, it seemed so long ago.

He went for his gun, but one of the brothers already had a weapon in his hand (a fleeting thought: he must've picked that Colt up someplace).

The man fired first.

Dachin's hat came off and he felt as if a redhot branding iron had been drawn across the crown of his head. Red – then going black – and then, strangely, he thought he heard hoofbeats. But maybe that was only the drumming of his own blood before the blackness came.

He came to his senses in a pale dawn. His head felt as if the top of it had been taken off. There were people around him but he couldn't see any of them till one bent over him, a broad face coming into focus. An anxious familiar face. His cousin, Bruke, who said, 'I wuz with the posse. I-I didn't know it was you, Clay. I didn't know.'

'Them two Mexicans. . . ?'

'They're both dead, Clay. They were crazy, put up a fight. . . .'

The voice faded and there was nothingness again.

A bullet had cut a channel across the top of his head.

The wound healed and gradually the scar became covered by his thick black hair.

The posse wanted to know where the bank loot was. He told them his partners had taken it with them and he didn't know where they were now. He said he couldn't remember where they had planned to meet.

They didn't believe much, but they couldn't do anything. It didn't occur to them to search the tumbledown shack.

Dachin knew that Jigger and Peaboy would keep out of the law's way. But he wouldn't be able to meet them, that was for sure. Somehow they would hear

113

what had happened to him.

He was tried quickly and sentenced to a stretch in Stark City.

He didn't see Jigger and Peaboy till they got him out of there, together with Bruke, though Dachin wouldn't have wanted Bruke involved. It seems however, that the big man had felt guilty about being in the posse that had captured his cousin. They'd been pretty clever, that posse.

So had, for a while, the Mexican brothers, picking up on Dachin as they had, although they had gone loco in the end and were now under the sod.

What headache Dachin might have had had been left behind in The Pit. Peaboy's ear still looked ragged if you took a closer peek at it, but it didn't bother him.

Now the three partners had to get the loot. As far as they knew, nobody else had. . . .

Part Three

THE LAST
SHOOT-OUT

EIGHTEEN

Before he could lead the other two on, Clay Dachin had a call to make. A very important one he said and there was, unusually, anxiety in his voice.

Jigger and Peaboy agreed to wait for him in a neighbouring settlement not far from his destination. He said he wouldn't be long, that this was just something he had to put right.

He did not tell them that, after they picked up the boodle and split it three ways, he aimed to take his cut, bid them goodbye and leave the owlhoot trail forever.

The settlement was a lonely place with no law. None of then knew anybody there.

The place of Dachin's destination was even lonelier.

From the narrow uneven trail that the rider and his horse followed the long one-storey cabin was sheltered and partially hidden by a grove of cottonwoods in the centre of which, Dachin knew, was a tiny spring, a small pool. He remembered that he and the dark, lovely girl, Della, used to lie sometimes beside that pool, out of the wind and in the shade where the short grass was soft and mossy, a natural bed.

He could see the corral. There were a few horses there. There was no other sign of life, no cooking smoke. The place was bathed in sunshine and there was a peaceful quietness except for the soft drumming of his horse's hoofs on the hard ground.

Usually Jabez Snow came out to greet visitors, a rifle or shotgun negligently sloped at his side. Just in case. . . .

Maybe Jabez was away. But where was the girl? She was friendly, but wary too, though this was not in any way a lawless territory. She had always affirmed that she could look after herself.

But was she herself now? He remembered the last time they had been together and what she had told him. Maybe both she and her father were away. But, if so, who tended the horses that were Jabez and his daughter's livelihood?

In his mind, Dachin tried to count the months and found himself confused, wary as he was and now in full sight of the cabin.

If those things hadn't happened. . . . His foolishness, his carelessness, his capture, the jail. Stark City and what had happened afterwards.

But here he was as he had planned, though much much later than he had planned.

He was startled when Jabez suddenly appeared in the cabin doorway, a rifle sloped at his side, his other hand raised, but in some subtle way as if to halt Dachin rather than greet him. Not a wave, or a hand outstretched in friendliness.

Jabez looked worn and old and the cabin looked uncared for, debris around the door and the windows. In the past, the man and his holdings had always been neat. Della had had a hand in that, a lovely, trim girl with a dazzling smile. Where was she?

Dachin reined in his horse but did not begin to dismount. 'How are you, Jabez?' he asked.

The older man didn't answer the question but said in a strangely toneless voice, 'You're alive. You've come back.' Statements of fact. Simple. Only calling for a simple 'Yes'. And then Dachin asked, as he would have to, 'Where is Della?' And a sudden dread assailed his heart as he looked into the lined face and the sad, tired eyes of this elderly man, his friend, his future father-in-law.

But not to be now!

'Della is dead.'

Then the story came out. In that grim, toneless voice.

'We didn't know where you were. Then we heard you were in jail. Then we heard you had been killed escaping from jail. There was a man who came to the settlement telling that tale and it was brought to us. Della wanted to go to the settlement to try and get the rights of it. I told her she mustn't, but I knew that if I went she would just follow me. She seemed to heed what I said. Two nags got out of the corral and I went after them, got them. Just a short way. But while I was out of sight she got the little gig and the pony and she took to the trail. . . .'

Jabez paused. Dachin saw him swallow. He hadn't moved, his hands by his sides, the rifle slack in one. Dachin sat his horse.

Jabez went on, 'We had a sudden flash storm, like

we get here now and then. I went out after Della. She was swollen with child. She shouldn't have been out at all. But now this. . . .

'I found her beside the trail in the rain and in the wreckage of the gig. The horse had bolted. He turned up in the settlement.' It was as if the grieving man at last wanted to get it all told, every tragic segment of it. 'She was dead. Her neck was broken.'

The voice died.

'I never knew,' said Dachin. 'I came as soon as a could. I made Della a promise—'

'I know. She told me.'

'I was going to ask you. . . .' Dachin's voice tailed off.

'Turn your horse about, Clay,' the older man said. 'I never want to see your face again.'

'I understand, Jabez.'

When he looked back he could only see the cotton-woods and the end of the house. He wondered whether Jabez was still standing at door, didn't think he was. He wondered who the man had been who had brought to the settlement the rumoured news that Clay Dachin, gunfighter and killer, was dead.

He remembered how Della used to ran around the edge of those cottonwoods when she came to meet him, her dark hair flying on her shoulders, her beautiful face so brilliantly alive.

That unknown rumour-monger and those before him had something to answer for but never would: their kind seldom did.

The tall man on the horse knew that he would

remember always the gentle, lovely girl who used to run around the cottonwoods to meet him: even in his great sadness that picture would stay with him and maybe, finally would comfort him.

He went back to Jigger and Peaboy. For himself he would rather have ridden on alone as if into nothingness. But he owed those two. And he was a man who always tried to pay his debts.

There was a debt he could not pay now and he thought he would carry that tragic knowledge with him forever – however long that might be.

NINETEEN

It had been an interrupted search. Hardly a search at all as far as Peaboy and Jigger were concerned, for they just did not know where to look.

To them, as well as to others – but to them most of all because he was their partner – Dachin was sometimes a complete enigma. And as changeable as the winds from the Gulf of Mexico that came across this part of the country.

Of a sudden, Clay Dachin seemed to have become obsessed about doing what was best, what was right and loyal, the complete *rightness* of things. He had insisted on staying for the funerals at Caliero, Hell's Back Door. He had marched with the mourners at the crowded burying of Juan, chief of the muleskinners, and had even showed himself at other buryings, sticking his neck out as his two partners had thought.

Maybe he was sort of cocking a snoot at Panama Jack and his minions. But right now Jack it seemed was singing small anyway. His right-hand man Billy Sarmo was out of commission. But mending well. Of Billy's two main partners who had taken part in the raid on the Stark City prison complex only one remained, Sep. Dan had been killed, his body brought back. Dachin even put in an appearance at that young man's burying.

Clay's cousin, big Bruke accompanied him on these short excursions, while Peaboy and Jigger lounged impatiently in the saloon. Bruke kept saying he was going back home, Clay urging him to do so. But hadn't gone yet.

The searching trio did manage to leave the big man behind when they finally set off on the trail again, wondering whether at last a force would descend on Hell's Back Door seeking to avenge the carnage that had engulfed Stark City. But the three partners, well, they had other things to do.

But Clay broke the trail again, leaving the other two waiting while he went off once more – a lonely loner.

When he returned he seemed even more a sad loner, and even quieter than he had ever been before.

Bruke's trail was a tortuous one. He figured that the boys wouldn't expect him to follow them. Clay had told him to go back home to his mother and the stores, had said he would have something for him later – whatever that was.

He figured that if the boys spotted him they would rein in and wait for him, if only to tell him to go home. It seemed to him that folks were always telling him to go home, as if he were a boy a bit simple in the head.

For a while, strangely enough, he thought that he, in turn, was being followed. But then the feeling left him. If there was somebody after him, he had shaken them off. Or maybe it was just that his imagination had been playing him tricks. He wasn't big on imagination, but he knew that if he really put his mind to work he could be a damn sight cleverer than folks gave him credit for.

More than anybody else in the world he trusted Clay, who had been like a brother to him in the old days. But he didn't know whether he trusted Peaboy and Jigger. Maybe those two were planning a double-cross on Clay.

Still and all, imagination or not, Bruke wasn't perfectly sure why he'd taken this trail: he just told himself that he was looking out for Clay the way Clay had always looked out for him.

He got sidetracked. And at one point Clay left his two partners on their own and went off a-riding.

At first Bruke didn't know what to do. Then he decided to wait. And he hunkered down in a little draw in sight of the settlement where he knew Peaboy and Jigger were waiting.

He saw Clay come back and he saw the trio leave and he took up the trail again. Clever? Oh, yes, he was being clever all right.

But he wasn't clever enough. Maybe he even outsmarted himself. He lost them!

Maybe they had at last spotted him, hadn't reckoned who he was, had thought him of no consequence, had shaken him off. Whether or not, he had lost their trail completely. Then, like a big hound dog who'd lost the scent he started to sniff around and try and pick it up again.

Back in the place that he had begun to think of as Hell's Back Door he had gotten friendly with Billy Sarmo and Billy had spotted him leaving, had wanted to ride along with him, if only for 'a breezer' as he put it. But Billy was still strapped up and the doc had told him to rest.

Bruke had thanked Billy for the offer but had dissuaded him, said he'd see Billy again although he wasn't sure that he ever would. Anyway, he wasn't keen on Billy's pards, including the young gunfighter called Sep whose pard, Dan, had been killed in Stark City – and afterwards Sep had latched on to Billy.

Bruke particularly disliked and mistrusted Panama Jack, although he knew Peaboy and Jigger – and Clay for that matter – had done business with the man, the broker, the go between, the fixer. Jack was by way of being Billy Sarmo's boss, though they didn't exactly seem to be seeing eye to eye lately.

Leaving those possibilities on one side, Bruke now began to wsh he had Billy with him, for that small, plump, cherubic hell-raiser had the reputation of being a mighty fine tracker.

Off-horse, Bruke bent and peered, even got down on his knees, while the patient beast took things easy at last, chewed a cud and watched his master quizzically, until the man turned and swore at him, something he didn't usually do. And the beast turned away, flicking his tail indignantly, showing the man his butt, sloped off a little further, seeking more inviting pasture.

'Don't go too far, jackass,' the man said.

Bruke had been sharpening his eyes, his wits also. Suddenly he became erect and looked about him, and his mind began to race as memory prodded him.

He had seen this territory before, been over it backwards and forwards. He had been with a posse and they'd been chasing a fugitive and he hadn't known that that fugitive was his own cousin – until the bunch caught up with Clay.

But Clay didn't have the boodle they had thought he'd have, and he'd told them that his two partners had it. And they'd believed him; they'd thought he hadn't had time to hide it, dig a hole for instance, cover it up.

A ghost town. And he had planned to hide in it.

At least, that was what they had thought.

'Come here, jackass,' Brute said. 'Sharp now.'

The cayuse reacted to his voice in part, but ambled. The man went up to him, mounted, pointed his now co-operative head in the right direction.

Yes, there were those low bluffs – he remembered them, the man thought.

He looked behind. Nothing moved back there. Nothing moved in front either, he thought . . . but I'll stake my davy.

But not too fast. . . . *Not too fast now.*

They hit a wider trail, but a much rockier and uneven one with all kinds of vegetation sprouting from it, creeping along it. The going became more perilous as night fell. Bruke wasn't too upset, however, realiz-

126

ing more than ever that his hunch – if it could be
called that – had been correct.

This was a trail that was rarely used now, had once
led to a thriving mining settlement which the last
time he saw it, had beome a ghostly shadow.

It must have deteriorated even more since then
with the elements which were not exactly placid over
this particular place on earth.

From time to time the big man halted his steed
and listened. And heard nothing but the usual night
noises. He became what his sainted mother would
have called cock-a-hoop. But this feeling was taken
from him suddenly in dramatic fashion. His horse hit
something on the trail and stumbled, almost pitch-
ing his rider's bulk from the saddle.

Bruke, regaining his balance, drew the beast to a
halt and dismounted carefully. In the light from the
pale moon, which had bloomed, he examined the
horse and discovered he had thrown a shoe.

He got back into the saddle and urged the beast
on with a click of the tongue, saying, 'See how you
go, ol' pard.'

But, very soon, he realized it was no go, and he
dismounted and led the limping beast off the rough
trail and on to softer ground. He led the horse, walking himself very awkwardly on high-heeled riding
boots. And the ground seemed to be getting as hard
as a rock plateau.

They rested. The man took a pull from his canteen
and wet a rag and laved the horse's mouth and nose.
He didn't want to lose his ol' pard, hoped to get him
to the settlement, though the journey was going to

take a hell of a lot longer than he'd expected, and more circuitous because they weren't using the trail.

They were resting again when the man thought he heard hoofbeats on the trail, the sound quickly fading into a near silence, night making him wonder whether he'd imagined things again, over-using his aching brain till it matched his aching body.

I didn't see anything, he thought. The pale moonlight made ghosts. Had he really heard something? He could've called out. Would it have been wise to call out? Nobody had seen him, heard him. . . .

The horse made a little snorting noise and Bruke realized he had spoken some of his thoughts aloud, though no words echoed in his aching brain. I'm moon-dazed, he thought, and it ain't much of a moon at that.

'All right, boy,' he said, and now he was talking in a soft voice to the horse. 'We'll make it all right. We'll make it.'

TWENTY

The three men's first sight of the ghost town had been in the twilight.

'Have we come to the right place?' Peaboy had asked.

'It's the right place,' Dachin said. 'But it's changed. It's worse.'

'Changed,' snorted Jigger. 'Hell, it's disappearing.'

There were shattered timbers on the outskirts, nothing that could be called a structure of any kind. And even as far as they could see – and the shadows were deepening – there was nothing that appeared upstanding. This was not even a ghost town now, just a scattered pile, or a succession of piles that had once been buildings of various sizes but were now in no way identifiable as such.

Dachin began to ride slowly around the edge of the ruins and the other two followed him. He paused at a grassy hump in the ground, a soddy that had fallen in on itself. Some impoverished person must have lived once in that veritable hole in the ground. There was a flat rocky patch in front of it blackened in places by old fires, but creeping vegetation was taking over.

'Was that the place?' Peaboy asked.

'Nothing like it,' said Dachin. 'It was a fallin'-down cabin.'

'We're surrounded by fallin'-down cabins,' said Jigger caustically. 'An' most of 'em are pretty nigh flat. An' spread by the wind.'

Peaboy began to laugh softly, a hollow sound.

'I've got to get my bearings,' Dachin said. 'But the light's getting worse.'

A pale moon was peeping, throwing an eerie light. The shadows were lengthening, getting thicker.

'Well, we're here anyway,' said Dachin. 'We better rest up an' take a better look by daylight.'

'That soddy, that'll be sheltered,' said Jigger, pointing. 'Place for a fire as well. I was born in a soddy like that.'

There was an opening for snide comments, but neither Dachin or Peaboy took advantage of this. And the former said, 'Yeh, might help me to get my bearings. Not as I remember seein' any damn' soddy time back. But I might spot somep'n else from there.' He turned his horse about. The other two followed his example, tailed him like two troopers on reconnoitre with the company sergeant.

They cleared the brush from the entrance of the soddy and Jigger being the smallest and the nosiest, crawled in first.

'More space than you'd think on,' he called, his

voice booming strangely. 'An' it don't stink none too bad.'

Peaboy followed, said, 'Phew! Like a polecat. You might be used to that, brother, but not me.' Getting his dig in at last.

Jigger said something that Dachin couldn't catch, but it sounded obscene. Ducking in, he said, 'We could clean it, get some dry sweet grass in here. We can light a small fire as well. It could be hidden from the main trail.'

'You think somebody might be follering us then?' said Peaboy.

'Who knows?'

They let Jigger do the work: he didn't seem to mind. Also, he was the one with the convenient tool which he'd brought along with him. A shovel in two parts which could be threaded together. He'd bought it for the price of a few drinks from a mule-skinner back in Hell's Back Door and Dachin had complimented him on his foresight.

He worked well and fast while Peaboy made a small fire and Dachin surveyed the terrain, what he could see of it under the pale moon.

The soddy finished habitable at least, no smellier than an early morning stable. Dachin said there was plenty of room for two and they would take turns at keeping watch outside. Peaboy had brewed coffee and they had some biscuits and hard tack. The horses were tethered in a bunch and hitched to a lone post, part of a door by the look of it, where among the shattered timbers there was some sweet grass. The night went on. A whippoorwill called. A coyote sang.

*

'We gotta rest up, ol' pard,' Bruke said to his horse. 'We've wandered too far off the trail an' I'm losing my sense o' direction.' He was consulting his battered gun-metal half-hunter. 'It's later than I thought. Maybe we'll get there by first light, likely. Anyway, I've gotta do somep'n for you, ain't I? Should've done it before I guess.'

He inspected the horse's foot again. It was sore from the absence of a shoe and there was a slight swelling above it. Bruke soaked in water the rag he had used before but this time tore in two strips and bound it gently around the sore place, his large hands deft and manipulative. The horse looked down, watching him, didn't make a sound.

Bruke hunkered down, took out his makings, rolled himself a quirley, lit up.

'Pity you cain't smoke,' he said to the horse.

The horse snorted.

At first light Clay Dachin walked on his own around what was left of the ghost town, looking about him all the time, near, and as far as he could reach, though that wasn't yet far, no moon now and the light a strange, smoky pearly-grey. Still, it was the near things that interested him most.

The two boys and he had had cover and a few eats and now Peaboy and Jigger were hunkered down by the dying fire, their first smoke of the day. The horses were grazing. Even among the ruins this was a peaceful scene.

Dachin kept pausing, staring at the ground now as if deep in thought. All he could see was rubbish.

It had seemed such a long time ago. . . .

And he had been in this place such a short time.

Finally, though, he waved to his partners, called them over. Jigger brought his shovel, its two parts screwed together, ready. Dachin pointed to the ground, to what was merely a pile of broken wood with weeds sprouting in probing fingers from it. 'Under there,' he said.

They found nothing. They moved on to another place. The sun came out. Its heat intensified. They were sweaty, disgruntled, staring downwards, dust in their eyes. Nothing else. There was space all around them, except for the rubbish grotesque under the sun. They did not keep a good watch, only when they straightened and wiped their faces: such a lot of rubbish to shift, wooden spars to lift with aching arms and shoulders, fingers full of splinters.

The other three men, coming in off the trail, had made a wide detour and entered the ghost town at the other side from Dachin and his two partners.

They had found some trees and left their horses there, entered the town on foot, using all the cover they could find. Like the men they had trailed they had rested too, in the night, hidden in the trees, watching the small light of the fire their quarries had made and which could be seen very easily from this side of the shattered town.

Now it was sunup, and later. They had expected to

pick up the loot right off, and leave three corpses behind. But the trio ahead had no loot. And there was frustration all round.

'Goddamn idiots,' said Panama Jack. 'They don't know where to look.'

'Do you?' snapped Billy Sarmo.

He still had his arm in a sling, had carried a sawn-off shotgun across the saddle in front of him, carried it loosely now in one hand.

Jack didn't answer Billy's question, and the third man kept silent: young gunfighter Sep whose partner, Dan, had been killed during the Stark City débâcle. Sep was along for pay, doing what he was told, figured this go-down had to be profitable or Jack, who usually stayed in his web like a skeletal spider, wouldn't have come out on the owlhoot trail.

'We'll just have to watch 'em,' Jack said, stating the obvious.

But Sep suddenly got impatient, rose a little from behind a pile of rotting timber to get a better look at he knew-not-what and Jigger, nervous as a cat, turned and spotted him.

Jigger gave an inarticulate cry and reached for his gun.

Billy Sarmo, who had raised himself a bit in order to remonstrate with Sep, lifted his shotgun, levelled it in one swift motion and let off a barrel.

Jigger was thrown, spun, a terrible wound high up in his side. He was dead before he hit the ground.

His companions, warned, hit the ground themselves, burrowing for cover. They had just about as much as the other three – but there was only two of *them* now. 'God'amighty,' said Peaboy and, reckless as ever, began to crawl towards his motionless friend. But, from his position, Dachin could see Jigger better and said, 'You can't do anything for him.' And Dachin's Colt bucked and flamed and boomed.

But Panama Jack and his two colleagues had found deeper cover. Dachin had spotted Billy Sarmo, thought, I should've figured this.

A bullet zipped past his cheek, threw splinters in his face. He couldn't see anything. Somebody had found a peephole. A trickle of warm blood ran down Dachin's face. What a bullet couldn't do, a sliver of jagged wood had managed to do, which was preferable. Dachin fingered the place. A long, narrow scratch, that was all.

Billy Sarmo let loose the second barrel of his shotgun, the report booming over the sharper notes of the handguns everybody else was using. No rifles were needed yet. Nobody was running.

Peaboy, steadying himself, had his left hand on wood while he lifted his right with the Colt in it. He cried out, dropping his left hand, it was gushing blood. Some of Billy's shot had taken the top off Peaboy's knuckles.

He thumbed the hammer of the handgun but the slug whined uselessly in the air. He held out his mutilated hand mutely towards Dachin who crouched only a few yards from him.

Dachin whipped the bandanna from around his neck, grabbed Peaboy's bloodsoaked paw, wrapped the cloth around it, tied it in a knot, using all his strength, his own handgun at his side for the moment.

The blood was stanched. 'Thanks, Clay,' said Peaboy.

He raised his gun again. Easy going Peaboy was all killer now, his teeth bared, his eyes squinting.

Shots were exchanged. Both sides were sending down a barrage. Billy Sarmo was using a handgun now, awkwardly. But no great marksmanship was needed. Neither side could see much to shoot at.

Dachin lifted a scrap of wood shaped like a small cross, threw it a little to the side of him, using his left hand, his gun half-lifted in his right fist, his thumb on the hammer.

Young Sep fired at the movement as the wooden cross fell, raising dust. His shot went wide of Dachin. But Sep showed himself and Dachin aimed, thumbed the hammer twice.

Both shots hit their target. One in Sep's shoulders jerking him upwards like a puppet on a string, the other in the side of his head, not exactly a plumb shot but a fatal one. Sep had time to scream; he spun, clawing at the air and then flopped forward over the jumbled wooden bulwark that had sheltered him. He was like a large, raggedy doll draped there, his hands dangling, becoming still.

Skeletal Panama Jack and his small, plump, cherub-faced sidekick were more seasoned gunslingers than the impatient Sep had been. Jack had, over the recent years, chosen a more sedate style of living, paying others to do his dirty work for him while he schemed his schemes and became notorious and well used as murder broker and go-between for anything nefarious and profitable.

Billy had spent much of his time gambling and chasing the girls who seemed to like his pink-cheeked charm. But he was a cold-blooded killer when he chose to be, often at his skeletal chief's behest.

Jack, an immensely greedy man, had chosen to take a leading role in this particular go-down, and Billy had been delighted to go along with him. Privately, Billy had figured that maybe Jack was sort of on his way out as far as an owlhoot job like this was concerned – and Billy wouldn't mind being top dog himself, not at all.

Billy, despite his somewhat effete appearance – some had challenged this and had not lived to tell the tale – had no fear in him. To him, going up against a notorious top gun like Clay Dachin was nothing more or less than a delightful challenge.

He had two handguns and he used them in turn, whooping shrilly from time to time, his plump face beaded with sweat and the oil of it running down from beneath his wide-brimmed felt hat. The sun was a blood-red ball and this was a battleground.

TWENTY-ONE

The small town didn't look like any town at all any more, not even a ghostly one. There weren't any structures that could still be called habitations, places of business, store-places, horse and other live pens and stables, outhouses and privies.

All had been shattered and flattened by the elements: the sun and rain and the winds from the Gulf, the bewildering and sometimes violent changes of weather that bedevilled this territory.

The town had been built on flat land with no shelter, though the grass hadn't been bad. The mines had been in the hills which were a distance away, not tall, no shelter to the town at all, the winds swirling the dust over and around them.

Near the town there was a narrow creek, the reason for the buildings being put there in the first place. A tributary of the Big Red, an infant which became dry in the hot summers so that the townsfolk had had to dig for water.

It was a strange spot for a pitched battle to be taking place.

The echoes rolled, the gunsmoke drifted over shattered timbers, a spar sticking up here and there like wreckage from a sunken ship, broken fingers trying to point at the sky, the smell of cordite, the whisper and haze of dust in the sun motes, the mocking echoes and the small wind under the blazing orb of the sun.

Billy Sarmo was using the sprawled, draped body of his late colleague, Sep, as a shield. Damaged as Billy was, he needed a prop for his handgun. He had always claimed to be a two-gun operator and he was proving it now, wasn't half-bad.

Billy was plump and sweating; Panama Jack was skeletal, a never-sweat. He hid himself well, like a snake. He crawled, his chin brushing the dust. He was unharmed. But now it looked as if he was trying to hide himself completely, disappear.

Billy Sarmo had a small bruise on his temple where, in his impatience he had knocked himself on a jagged baulk of timber.

More bullets thudded into the inanimate body of young Sep. Billy grinned devilishly. His sweat and dust-spotted face was no longer cherubic and his exposed teeth were as feral as a wild fox's.

A man down on each side and, although Jack and Billy didn't know it, Peaboy with a mutilated left hand, blood seeping through the improvised bandage.

Nausea was beginning to overtake Peaboy and, with it, a burning rage.

'Let's take 'em,' he screamed and he rose and clambered, long-legged, over the sprawled and criss-

139

crossed timbers that had sheltered him. He marched forward, gun blazing. And Billy Sarmo appeared.

They were both kind of crazy. They were both good shots, though, conditioned: that was the way of them.

Peaboy's left arm dangled at his side, the blood from his shattered hand spattering the dust and the timbers, defiling the small patches of green grass.

He was hit in the shoulder, spun around by the drive of the slug. It was closer quarters now. He did not fall. His eyes glared and power drove him.

And Billy was hit too. A bullet in his good shoulder had made him drop his gun on the back of the still form that had been his shield. He scrabbled for the weapon, grasped it with desperation, managed to lift it. But slowly as if it were an anvil. He was hit again, high in the chest, a killing blow. But his trigger finger contracted and the gun bucked in his hand.

Panama Jack hadn't risen. His lean white face peeped. He was shooting at Clay Dachin who, although taken by surprise by Peaboy's pain-induced, rage-filled and desperate ploy, was now advancing, gun levelled and flaming.

Billy, the life gone from him, was lying across the corpse of Sep as if in a last embrace.

Billy's last involuntary shot had been a lucky one, the bullet speeding to its target which Billy hadn't been able to see any more. Peaboy, like Billy, had taken the bullet in the chest and was flat on his back, a bullet that Panama Jack had also flung at him going harmlessly across his body as the last breath of life was emitted from his desperate mouth.

And, suddenly, then, Panama Jack was running.

Dachin was down on one knee, evading Jack's last shots, gazing at the dead face of his friend, Peaboy, which seemed to have smoothed into a sort of handsome resignation.

Dachin was startled by Jack's sudden about-face, snapped a couple of shots but knew he had missed. The thin man, half-crouching, weaving, was not a good target.

On the periphery of Dachin's vision another figure appeared, raised a rifle to a shoulder, aimed, fired. But Jack kept on running, disappeared in the shelter of some trees.

Dachin had turned sideways. He lowered his gun. He had recognized the big man with the rifle. His cousin Bruke. A surprise. But there he was, unmistakable – larger than life as usual.

Back behind Bruke, though not near the trees, a horse stood.

Then another horse broke from the trees and this one had a rider. And the rider was Panama Jack. Dachin raised his handgun but then lowered it again, knowing he was way out of range. At the slam of hoofs, Bruke turned fully around and raised his rifle to his shoulder again, levelled it.

Jack was low over the saddle, crouched, looped over the other side of his horse from the rifleman.

To Dachin, the crack of the rifle sounded like a whiplash, the echo then rolling back and dying to a nothingness.

The galloping horse kept going. The crouching man stayed in the saddle. Bruke swung the muzzle of the rifle in a short arc, aiming again. But then he lowered it as if in disgust, a shrug of his big shoulders.

Jack was out of range, going like the wind. He was higher in the saddle now, seemed unharmed, didn't look back.

If only one of us had had a long range Sharps, Dachin reflected. Bruke was coming forward, his broad face wearing an anxious expression. The browsing horse began to follow the big man and Dachin saw that the beast was lame.

They found two more horses in the trees, led them out.

Dachin said, 'We've got to cover these bodies before we go after Jack. We know where he'll go anyway – back to his friends in Caliero, the folks who'll back 'im.'

They covered Jigger and Peaboy well with timber and Dachin said, 'I'd like to pick 'em up later, take 'em back for a proper funeral.'

They covered Billy and Sep in the same way. They could stay where they were forever as far as Clay and Bruke were concerned, silent now.

But as they got ready to hit the trail Bruke said, 'My hoss, he ain't fit.'

'Take him down to the creek and leave him there. Grazing and sustenance a-plenty. You can pick him up later.'

'All right. I'll take the saddle an' everything off. He won't need that weight.'

Bruke took one of the spare horses. They let the

others follow them.

As they rode, Bruke said, 'So you didn't find what you were lookin' for?'

'No.'

'You don't seem to care.'

'No. I guess I don't. Too much has happened, old *amigo*. Too much of much.'

'I know what you mean.'

'Yeh, you'd know.' It was a compliment from Clay to a man who had been like a brother to him, a man whom he had looked after – and was now returning the compliment, would carry on doing so. And now Clay Dachin knew that he could not dare try and shut the big, intensely loyal fellow out of this. He knew that Bruke had always been mighty good with a rifle, would want a chance to prove that after missing out back at the ghost town.

There would be ghosts there now all right: it was a sad thought.

And retribution would have to be taken.

Dachin did not plan ahead past that. The future was in the laps of whatever ornery Fates took a hand in such things.

He knew that Bruke would be with him till the end, and that was sufficient to him as they rode to their grim destination.

Hell's Back Door.

TWENTY-TWO

It was an outlaw town, a stopping place for desperados from over the border, evading their law. A stopping place and hideout for miscreants from the Norteamericano side too, who could slip over the border if their own law was on their tails.

It had its own population, however, venal or otherwise. And it had its leading citizens, none any better than they should be. Anglos, Mexicans, *mestizos* who were half-Mex half-Indian, other 'breeds of all kinds of permutations, tribal Indians who had become halfway civilized, a few blacks who had once been slaves: a mess and mixture of humanity.

Some thought of Panama Jack as a sort of leading citizen. There were others, mainly of the Mexican and allied contingent who had thought of the mule-skinner leader Juan as a leader, and a wise one. But Juan wasn't with them any more, had died during the débâcle at Stark City and his colleagues missed him greatly, as did various other *peons, vaqueros, caballeros*, Indians and the like to whom he had become an uncle, even a father figure.

The Stark City raid had taught them that Juan could lead them into a sort of independence and, although Juan wouldn't have wanted it wholly that way, they held on desperately, pugnaciously to that independence; and the gap between them and the likes of Panama Jack and his minions became wider.

And then there was a thought at the back of everybody's mind that a form of retaliation might still ultimately come from the direction of Stark City, in ruins though it now was. It would not be the first time that Anglo law or the military had descended on Caliero.

Some folks, mainly male, drifted on over the border. But the townsfolk stayed. It was their town after all. They knew the nickname that had been given to it by the law and the lawless. But, if it was hell it was their own kind of hell and they laughed in the face of the devil.

It was known that Panama Jack had left Hell's Back Door, taking with him the baby-faced young killer Billy Sarmo and another man even younger, less well known than the notorious Billy but of the same stripe.

Not a bunch. Just three men. But probably there was money the end of it and a three-way split was a lip-licking one: skeletal Jack's insatiable greed was legendary. He would torture and kill for money.

When Panama Jack came back it was still day, though the light was failing. He was alone, and that was a surprising thing. Or was it? Had Jack double-crossed his companions, backshot them, left them out in the badlands? The *peons* and the muleskinners wondered.

And Jack's own people were speculative too, particularly those who had wanted to go with him on the trip, had felt left out. Jack looked harassed: they fed on that among themselves, but they didn't do or say anything to his face.

His skull face was as inscrutable-looking as ever. But there seemed to be a haunted – or *hunted* – look in his evil eyes – could anybody say that?

In truth, Jack himself thought afterwards that he should have waited till dark before he entered the town. He'd shown himself to too many people. But then it was too late and he began to make his plans.

He lived in the biggest house in the town, one he'd had built to his own specifications, and it was like a fortress. This was his base for his network: his moneylending (at exorbitant rates), his planning of jobs for his own men and others (his terms were high), his girls (he owned all kinds of establishments), his own spiderweb spin-offs.

He had folks watching. . . .

He had folks watching more than ever now.

Dachin and Bruke waited till nightfall and a quietening down before easing along to the outskirts of Caliero.

They had not left anything valuable in the ruins of the ghost town, except maybe the loot that had brought about all the conflict and trouble and tragedy. Maybe some old prospector or a couple of kids playing hookey, getting lost, had found the bundle. That was a comical thought.

Maybe some predators had eaten it! That was even more comical.

They had enough weapons to start a small war, which is what they aimed to do.

Something like that.

They had four spare horses, complete with saddles and other gear, a rattle-trap of accoutrements.

Actually, they had been later off the trail than they had at first expected to be. This was because Dachin had had a sudden gruesome idea and had insisted on returning to the ghost town.

At that time they had been barely halfway through the length of their journey back to Hell's Back Door and, although Bruke was in two minds about the proposed scheme, he went along with Clay as he always had done.

Bruke had a sense of humour, though, and later he began to appreciate the ghoulish and justifiable comedy of the scheme. And the bodies of Billy Sarmo and his new friend Sep had been uncovered and draped over the saddles of two of the spare horses and the now-cortège set off again.

There was still some noise coming from the low dives but all in all the town was pretty quiet, the streets deserted under the pale moonlight. Lights had gone out one by one. Some lights would stay on till the dawn, but they were in the minority. The denizens of the dens would be no problem.

The corpses of the two gunfighters had been taken down from where they had been draped across the backs of the two horses but now were being lifted back up there. They were being tied upright in the saddle with rawhide cut into lengths by Bruke's formidable jack-knife.

The two men worked deftly and, when they were finished the horses had riders in the saddle and, as if they had finally began to enter into the spirit of the game, were raring to go.

But there were still two riderless spare horses and they were to go first. A sort of incentive.

Dachin and Bruke's own two mounts were back a little, hidden behind a ruined privy which didn't smell as badly as it used to do, had spars of wood sticking out from it where reins could be looped.

The bunch, horses and men, faced downwards to the main street. The riderless cayuses were sent in first, their flanks slapped with pistol-like impact and, for good measure, a single shot fired from a gun over the beasts' heads, setting them at a furious gallop.

And, after that, the steeds with the mounted corpses needed no urging, set off in hot pursuit.

The men took to the shadows of the sidewalks, one on each side. Panama Jack's place was about halfway down main street, no light in its windows. But neither of the two men were fooled by this. They did not go too fast, however: there was a waiting, if moving, stealth about them, Bruke in particular moving very lightly for so big a man; he always had.

Ahead of them, near Jack's place, a gun went off. By this time the four horses, two of them with 'riders' were almost abreast of the doors and windows. A light went on in the upper floor: one of the tonier places, Jack's place with two stories, the toniest.

The four horses went on, their riders bobbing in the two saddles.

More lights were appearing in other directions.

A man came out of a dark doorway, gun raised, levelled at the rear of the four horses. Dachin came upon him and the man's instincts made him turn. Dachin slashed him across the temple with a gun-barrel and he hit the sidewalk, became still.

Bruke was shepherding two curious elderly folk back into their home. They weren't arguing.

Down by the Panama Jack abode there was more shooting. One of the bodies tied to a saddle was hit, probably more than once, and became loose, began to swing back and forth as if a wind had caught it.

But there was no wind. There was the pale moon-light and blossoming lamplight, wisps of smoke and the smell of cordite.

Somebody shouted that the town was being raided, as such could be the case. Should the towns-folk defend themselves, or should they stay in bed, their heads beneath the clothes?

TWENTY-THREE

Old Lorenzo ran a cantina in a long, low building. He was helped by his two sons. As Lorenzo was a widower and not a very good cook, the cooking was done by the as yet childless wife of one of the sons: the other one wasn't married.

The building belonged to Panama Jack. Old Lorenzo paid him rent, which was getting higher all the time. Lorenzo would have liked to own the place, lock, stock and barrel. But he couldn't make it. Leave it to his sons, that would be the great thing. But they couldn't make it either, though they did other things to try and help. They were good, hardworking boys.

That night, four of Panama Jack's hardcases woke them up, after everybody else had gone, and took over the place. Three men near the windows at the front, one at the back.

Old Lorenzo was still mourning for Juan, head muleskinner, who been his greatest friend. Lorenzo's daughter-in-law had only just got back from helping Juan's wife and the two kids.

She was shepherded into the back with Lorenzo

and the two boys. Jack's men had collected all the weapons they could find.

The thudding of hoofs began and Lorenzo and his two boys exchanged glances and moved. The hard-case in the kitchen watching the back was slugged on the back of the head with a fire-log in the fist of a moccasined boy, didn't know what had hit him, while the father was lifting a floorboard under a mat in the sitting-room and bringing out a shotgun and two pistols. In his youth, Lorenzo had been a border *bandido*; and you didn't forget the old tricks like always having hidden firepower.

The hardcases didn't have much chance. No tough trio were ever so surprised!

One of them tried – and got shot in the leg. The other two gave up without more trouble. After all, they were just hired hands who had been carrying out orders and there had already been an uneasiness among them about the way their boss had returned alone and was skulking now in his fortress.

The hardcases were quickly bound and the daughter-in-law stood over them with a shotgun while the old man and his sons ventured abroad. They had plenty fire-power now.

They almost ran afoul of Bruke, who had taken up a post opposite Panama Jack's place. Clay Dachin had already gone up an alley opposite and round back of the two-storey, fortress-like building. It was Bruke's job to keep folks pinned down. He had a rifle and was good with it.

Lorenzo and the boys spread out each side of him. They had to make sure they didn't shoot Dachin if he came right through. They knew the lean gunfighter by sight – as so did plump, quickshooting con-man Kelley Rodd when he turned up. And there were Mexican folk with various weapons. And an Indian with a huge old weapon that looked like a blunder-buss.

In Jack's place, the boys were automatically moving to the front. The thundering horses had gone by. There was no sound of hoofs now, only guns; and calling people. One of the boys said he'd hit a rider but the man had stayed in the saddle as if he'd been roped there. And that was a strange thing. Two riderless horses also. . . .

It was Jack who went to the back – as Dachin had expected him to do. Although Jack had had no hand in dubbing this township Hell's Back Door – who had, who knew? – he was certainly a back-door-type merchant himself.

Although Jack didn't know it, the two men he had placed on guard at the back, after being distracted by the sound of galloping hoofs and shooting out front, had been bushwhacked by Dachin, slugged, laid low. He was rising, half-crouching, from one of them whom he'd had to strike again, when Jack came through the back door with a gun in his hand.

Jack raised the gun and fired. He should have waited for Dachin to fully straighten: as it was, he only took the man's hat off. Dachin, momentarily off-balance, fired from his half-crouching position and he missed too. The slug took a chunk of timber out of the door-jamb behind Jack's head. Jack was coming forward, somewhat off-balance himself. His gun bucked in his hand. The shot went wide and it was as if there was a sudden silence; then the speeding slug was awakening the echoes, ricocheting from something, whining away into nothingness.

Jack lashed out desperately with his gun and caught Dachin with a glancing blow on his unprotected skull.

Dachin slumped downwards over the prone body of one of the look-out men he had slugged.

Jack ran, a scarecrow shambling figure in the pale moonlight.

Dachin scrambled upwards, the pain in the side of his head threatening to push him down again like the weight of an anvil. He realized he still had his gun in his hand; and he lifted it.

Jack was like a wavering ghost, a spook-thing. Dachin took a shot at the strange, moving figure and knew he had missed. Then the figure disappeared.

Dachin came fully upright with a rush. He staggered against the wall beside the open kitchen door, heard gunshots which seemed a long way away. He felt blood running down his cheek, remembered he'd been hit before back in the ghost town. Fleabites! He was spurred on. He moved forward, hugging the wall a bit. Would Jack stay and fight?

Jack came out into the pale light. Had he been hiding? Or had he just reappeared as if by magic?

The two men fired simultaneously. But then Dachin's rapid second bullet, his Colt thumb-hammered, sped on the tail of his first one, no handshake in between, both slugs boring into Jack's chest with only a fraction of space between them. And the whole length of the man's skeleton form toppled, the legs coming up like flailing branches; and then the heels hitting the sod.

Jack lay still, his gun lying neatly at his side as if placed there in a peaceful manner by a grieving hand.

Dachin inspected a hole in his jacket which had flapped outwards on the right-hand side as he had lifted his gun-arm. There was a neat hole through the scuffed leather. Good job that wasn't across my gut at the time, Dachin reflected.

He went to Jack who looked surprised but strangely peaceful. Dachin pulled the lids over the questioning eyes then turned and went up the alley.

Jack's boys were lined up in the street, were being disarmed, an array of levelled guns keeping them still. They had given in – just hired hands after all!

Dachin and Bruke were riding in the early morning light.

Dachin said, 'They'll clean things up all right back there.'

Bruke said, 'They surely will.'

They were silent for a while. The sun was pushing through a pearly sky.

Bruke asked, 'What will we do with Jigger an' Peaboy?'

'We'll bury 'em there 'stead o' taking 'em back. I dunno, I think they'll appreciate that.'

'Maybe their spirits'll wander,' said Bruke, 'an' find the gold at last.'

Dachin looked hard at his cousin. He was finding

new things about the big man all the time. He did not say anything.

And then, a short time later, Bruke went on, 'Y'know, Clay, Mom an' me have been thinking for some time about selling up that place and goin' to California. Maybe take up something else. A horse place mebbe – I'm good with the nags, you know that.'

'Yeh, you are. And it'd certainly be better than pushin' flour an' bacon.'

'Yeh . . .' Bruke went on haltingly, 'You ever thought o' doin' somep'n like that, Clay?'

'Yes, I have to admit that lately I've thought along those lines. I've certainly worn out my welcome in this territory.'

'California maybe?'

'California sounds fine,' Dachin said.

They rode on in silence, each with his thoughts. The sun burgeoned. The ruined ghost town came into view. But it didn't look quite so bad now. . . .

AFTERMATH

Not much remained of the desert penal settlement known as Stark City. The denizens of Caliero which lay on the edge of the badlands and the border did their foraging well. The big clean-up. Also a sort of cloud of mystery descended on the desolate blackened place, enveloped it. No sort of vengeance was attemped against the Caliero folk who had taken part in the downfall of the ominous area. News appertaining to Stark City was sparse even in the Eastern papers which were notorious for printing highly coloured, horrendous reports about the Wild West. Maybe certain powers-that-were preferred things that way. Too many pertinent questions might be asked. Too many reputations might be put at risk.

Besides, the all-powerful ruler of Stark City – one Captain Hector Ezekial Stark – seemed to have vanished as if the ground had opened up and swallowed him. As well it might have done.

The town of Caliero became what might be termed halfway respectable, not living up so much to its nickname of Hell's Back Door. There were not a whole lot of new faces there. Escaped prisoners and many folk who had prices on their heads roamed abroad. Not many were captured. Some were caught for other things rather than being merely escapees. They had gone back too soon into their old ways. Shots were exchanged. Bodies swung in the breeze.

Soon the borderlands seemed to slumber as if waiting for something.

A slave-driving section boss known merely as Stuker joined the railroad crews that were building the silver lines across the West. He (Stuker) had his throat cut to the top of his backbone while lying abed one night. Nobody was indicted for the murder but papers found in the dead man's coat identified him as Hector Ezekial Stark. He should of course have destroyed this evidence long since. But he had once been so proud of that name ('the Captain') which had given him so much standing and an almighty power.

Maybe one of his old misused prisoners had caught up with him last. . . .

Maybe one of the workers – might he, or they, be Chinese, Dutch, German, Italian – had gotten fed-up with Mr Suker's slave-driving ways.

Clay Dachin, with his aunt and his cousin Bruke, moved to California. The trio began a horse ranch. Dachin and Bruke were good wranglers and the latter's mother a prime householder and business-woman. Dachin, still a fiddlefoot but legitimate all the way now, did the outer buying and selling, was away from the spread from time to time. A handsome and genial man, he had many female 'friends', like a drummer with fine lines in goods. He never, however, brought one of his lady friends back to the horse ranch with him.

When he was not travelling or doing his ranch chores he sat in his room and wrote industriously on long yellow papers. Eventually he made a visit to a publisher in New York and came back with good news.

Months later, Clay Dachin's autobiographical novel of the West was published. He had called it *The Big Hoosegow*, and on a flyleaf an inscription read *Dedicated to the memory of Della*.